Lion Lost & Found

Ghost Cat Shifters, Book 2

By J. H. Croix

This is a work of fiction. Names, characters, businesses, places, events and incidents are either the products of the author's imagination or used in a fictitious manner. Any resemblance to actual persons, living or dead, or actual events is purely coincidental.

ISBN: 1533290202
ISBN 13: 9781533290205

Dedication

To second chances - in life and love.

Sign up for my newsletter for information on new releases!

http://jhcroix.com/page4/

Follow me!

jhcroix@jhcroix.com
https://twitter.com/JHCroix
https://www.facebook.com/jhcroix

Centuries ago in the northern Appalachian Mountains, mountain lions fled deeper and deeper into the mountains, seeking safety from the rapid encroachment of humanity into their vast territory. Mountain lions developed the power to shift from human to mountain lion and back again, saving their species as they hid in plain sight. The majestic wild cats became creatures of myth in the East while they flourished out West. Everywhere they were known as ghost cats because they were rarely encountered in the wild and moved with prowess and stealth. The wild cats expanded their range as their shifter ancestors intermingled with them, deepening the circle of protection for the species with layer upon layer of secrecy. The infamous ghost cats had powers of stealth beyond what most people imagined. Yet, their safety relied on a contract that couldn't be broken among shifters—they must protect the secret of their existence. In recent years, this contract had weakened due to the greed and misplaced pride of a few shifters. The unprecedented success of shifters at hiding in plain sight over centuries had emboldened some who thought secrecy was no longer necessary.

Chapter 1

"Hey Vivi!"

Vivian Sheldon turned in the direction of the voice calling her name and spotted a table full of tipsy college students. She quickly grabbed a tray from the counter and set to pouring several house draft beers. She knew if she showed up to the table with only one, she'd be turning right back around for more.

Within moments, she slipped from behind the bar at Quinn's Restaurant and Bar and carried her tray to the table in question. Her foresight in bringing extra beers was rewarded with a hefty tip.

"Thanks Vivi! You're a mind reader," one of the guys declared as she turned away.

She offered a quick grin and headed back behind the bar. She worked pick-up shifts at Quinn's usually a few nights a week. She'd have preferred not to because the hectic pace could be tiring, but she always needed the money. As a single mother to her seven-year old daughter, Julianna, she tended to barely scrape by month-to-month. She loved her small landscaping business, but working at

Quinn's filled the gaps during slow months. If it weren't for her mother babysitting for free whenever she needed it, she didn't know what she'd do.

Quinn's was packed tonight, which was its usual state. Quinn's had been a fixture in Painter, Colorado for many years. It served classic pub fare with some modern updates to the menu in terms of more creative burgers and other items. It catered to pretty much everyone from the college students to locals and tourists who passed through town for skiing in the winter and hiking in the summer.

Vivi slipped behind the bar again, which ran the full length of the back wall. She quickly wiped down a spill on the polished wooden counter, its surface worn and grooved from years of use. She moved on to serving customers who lined the bar, occasionally glancing around the room to see if any tables needed drinks. Round tables were scattered throughout the center of the large room with booths lining the walls. Pool tables and card tables were through an archway to another room.

The night passed by quickly. By the time Vivi walked out at midnight, she had earned enough in tips to pay her electric bill. She stepped out into the cool autumn air and took a slow breath. The streetlights lining Painter's streets were on, lighting her way home. Painter, Colorado was a small town nestled in the Rocky Mountains. Vivi didn't live far from downtown, so she usually walked to and from work. She stood on the sidewalk for a moment before she began walking, the noise from Quinn's gradually fading as she made her way toward home.

She passed by mostly darkened storefronts with a few restaurants and bars still open. Painter was home to a state university and a ski resort, without which the small town would be a sleepy mountain hideaway. She'd forgotten to bring a jacket and shivered in the cooling air.

Lion Lost & Found (Ghost Cat Shifters)

Autumn in the Colorado Rocky Mountains could mean somewhat warm days and rather chilly nights with the temperature varying from day to day until winter took hold. She heard footsteps in the distance approaching her. Her senses sharpened, and she scented the man following her. He wasn't a shifter, which was a relief because it meant if she needed to she could easily fend him off. The downside was she might potentially terrify him.

Vivi had been born a mountain lion shifter into a family of shifters. Shifters blended easily into the world, shifting only when necessary or when desired. Painter happened to be a stronghold for shifters out West, but shifters were scattered throughout the country with clusters in some areas. They had many advantages in the West since wild mountain lions existed in healthy populations here. If a shifter in lion form was sighted in the forest, they were assumed to be a wild mountain lion. Back East, where mountain lion shifters were born out of desperation to save their kind, there was a different set of challenges since mountain lions were believed extinct in the East. Since secrecy was important for shifters, Vivi never took her safety for granted. Revealing herself was something she only did when she chose. She hoped it wouldn't be necessary now as she listened to the footsteps getting closer and closer.

Just when she considered it might be best if she ducked into one of the open bars up ahead, a man walked out of the very door she'd been eyeing. Heath Ashworth's profile was instantly recognizable to her. A breath of relief washed through her. She'd known Heath for just about forever. He stood in the shadowed light and glanced around, his eyes narrowing when he saw her. He immediately turned toward her and began walking in her direction, his stride long and loose. As he approached, he caught her eyes. "Wait here," he said as he walked past her.

She stopped on the sidewalk and turned to look behind her. The man who'd been following her slowed as Heath approached him. Heath leaned over and spoke in the man's ear. Now that she was close enough, she could see the man was young and clearly intoxicated. He swayed back and forth on his feet as he stood in front of Heath. Heath stood tall again. When the man remained where he was, wobbling slightly, Heath gently placed his hands on the man's shoulders and turned him around. With a little push, the man began walking back down the sidewalk. As he passed by a lighted bar, he turned and stumbled through the door.

Heath turned around and walked back, coming to a stop in front of her. Her pulse started to race, and she tried to tamp it down. Heath was her best friend's older brother, and she'd fought a crush on him since they were teenagers. At thirty-two years old, Heath was three years older than she and her best friend Sophia. Vivi had hidden her crush from Sophia all those years ago and somehow managed to convince herself it was over when Heath enlisted in the Marines and left Painter. She rarely saw him, except for his brief visits home, for many years. About a year and a half ago, he came home for good.

In the years Heath was gone, she'd tried to bury her youthful crush and fancied herself in love with Julianna's father. That had turned out to be nothing more than a case of some serious wishful thinking. After Julianna was born, her father quickly faded out of sight. For the first few years of Julianna's life, he popped up here and there, but Vivi hadn't heard from him in over three years. She'd learned her lesson well and hadn't dated in years.

Right here, right now, in downtown Painter, Heath stood before her and every fevered fantasy she'd had about him when she was a teenager came roaring to the fore. Heath was all kinds of tall, dark and mysterious, even though she'd known him as long as she could remember. He had a body of pure muscle with the simmering power of a mountain lion shifter. His dark hair teased the edges of the denim jacket he wore. His green eyes flicked down to hers.

Okay, Vivi. Now would be the time to get a hold of yourself. You cannot start wishing for the impossible. Heath is not interested in you, so don't give yourself any crazy ideas. As soon as she finished that thought, she glanced up into his eyes again and what she saw there made her wonder. If it were anyone other than Heath, she'd have sworn she saw desire darkening his gaze. But this was Heath, and she was nothing more than an overworked single mother barely getting by and his sister's best friend who he treated with the same brotherly affection.

"Don't think that guy meant any harm. He's young and drunk and saw a pretty girl walking down the street," Heath said.

His husky voice was like a rough caress. It sent hot shivers through her. She tried to focus on what he said. "Oh, right. Yeah, I wasn't too worried, but I'm glad you happened to be around."

Heath nodded. "Wouldn't have thought you'd be worried," he said with a half-smile. "It's not your style."

She bit her lip and tried, oh she tried, to get her body to behave. But it was as if flames had encircled them. The air was so cool, and she was so hot inside. Heat suffused her and her pulse kept racing unchecked, no matter how hard she tried to slow it. She shivered at the contrast. Heath's eyes narrowed before he shrugged out of his jacket.

"You're cold. Here, this'll help."

He stepped closer to her and swung the jacket over
her shoulders, his arms caging her as it settled around her.
The denim was warm and held his scent. She had to close
her eyes to try to gain control of the desire surging through
her. When she opened them again, he was still there, inches
away from her. His hands had come to rest on her upper
arms. He slid them down, his touch sending an electric
current swirling through her. Her pulse rocketed and her
breath became shallow when she met his eyes.

His palms reached her hands, which were cold. His
hands, warm and strong, curled around hers, imparting his
heat to her. Just when she wondered what she should say to
snap this moment, he freed one of her hands and took a step
closer. He was so close now that when she took a breath,
her breasts rose and brushed against his chest. She flushed
straight through when she realized he could feel her peaked
nipples through her t-shirt. Something flickered in the back
of his eyes. Before she could ponder it, he slid his hand into
her hair and dipped his head.

When his lips were but a fraction away from hers,
he whispered, "I've been wanting to do this for too damn
long."

She was so stunned by his words, her jaw went
slack and her knees wobbled. His lips met hers, and any
pretense of thought dissolved into the desire pounding
through her. He didn't hesitate. He fit his mouth over hers,
and she lost her mind. At her gasp, his tongue swept inside
and need thundered through her. She arched into him and
moved entirely on instinct, so overtaken by sensation that
she couldn't think. Her tongue slid against his as she kissed
him with everything she had. His arm slipped around her
back and pulled her against him. She felt the heat of his
erection pressing into her belly. Hot, liquid need pooled
between her legs. She slid her hands up his chest, savoring

the feel of his hard muscles under her touch.

The sound of a car coming down the street filtered into her consciousness. The bright headlights arced across them. Heath tore his lips free. Awareness slid through her. She scrambled to gather herself. When she looked up, Heath's eyes were right there waiting. *Oh my God, oh my God, oh my God! What the hell were you thinking? You kissed Heath! You have to play it cool somehow. Probably means nothing to him. Take a nice deep breath and...*

Heath's hand loosened in her hair, and he slowly freed it before brushing a lock away from her forehead and tucking it behind her ear. Every touch struck sparks under the surface of her skin.

His eyes were somber as he looked down at her. He appeared to be considering his words. Frantic, she filled the silence. "Look, that was just a kiss. We weren't thinking. You don't need to worry I'll..."

He shook his head sharply. "I wanted to kiss you," he said bluntly. "You don't have to brush it off."

She hadn't realized she'd been holding her breath until it came out in a whoosh. Her hands were still on his chest, and she could feel the fast beat of his heart under one of her palms. "Oh, um... Oh."

Wow, brilliant, Vivi. Think you could say 'oh' one more time?

She mentally sighed and glanced up again. His eyes held a glint of amusement, but he was quiet. She took a deep breath, the cool air soothing her nerves just enough so she could think. "Okay. This is, uh, unexpected, and I'm not sure what you're thinking."

"I'm thinking what I said. I've wanted to kiss you for too damn long, so I finally did."

***

Heath looked down at Vivi, his heart pounding so hard, it reverberated through his body. She took another breath, which nearly broke his control again. He could only take so much of the feel of her tight nipples against his chest. They were on Main Street in downtown Painter in full view of anyone who drove by. He wasn't sure if he'd lost his mind by kissing her, but he wasn't going to lie. If there was one thing he'd learned in the last year and half, honesty was the only thing that would keep his head above water.

Vivi's dark hair fell around her shoulders. It gleamed where the streetlights caught it. Her blue eyes were bright against her fair skin. His eyes roamed over her face—the arch of her brows, her high cheekbones slanting down to her bow-shaped mouth, and the subtle vulnerability hiding deep in her eyes. It was that which made his heart clench. He remembered Vivi when she was younger, almost always with Sophia, and so bold, brash and bright. When he returned to Painter after over a decade in the military, it was as if her light had dimmed. He hadn't known how much he counted on seeing her spark until it wasn't so bright.

What he'd said was true. Many years ago, he'd had a few youthful fantasies about her, but he'd swatted them away. It wasn't exactly kosher to lust after his little sister's best friend. A decade in the military had pushed any fantasies far out of his mind. The last year had nearly broken him. A life-changing car accident sent him to the hospital. He'd left the hospital and cycled through several surgeries to repair his shattered femur. In a fog on painkillers, he'd stumbled around. Occasionally when the fog lifted, he'd see Vivi and wish he could have a chance to explore the fierce pulse of desire he felt for her. Until the last few months when he'd been forced to face his accidental painkiller addiction and how low it brought him, he hadn't felt worthy of anyone. Most certainly not worthy of Vivi—she was strong, loyal, caring, and simply spectacular. Doubt flickered in his mind. Being a shifter, doubt wasn't something he was accustomed to. Yet, this last year had weakened him in ways he'd never imagined. He felt strong again, but he wasn't sure he was worthy of Vivi.

"Maybe I wanted to, but maybe I shouldn't have done that," he said abruptly, the words coming out before he considered them.

Vivi's eyes slammed into his. "Why do you say that?"

He cleared his throat, trying to stay focused. "Because I messed up this year. Big time. You don't need…"

Vivi's eyes flashed in the glimmer from the streetlights. "Don't you dare go there! So you messed up? Once, only once, after a hellish year and all kinds of pain. You've already made it out the other side. You're a shifter, you're too strong to do anything other than rise above. You already have and you're a better man for it." She paused and took a shaky breath. "Maybe I have all kinds of questions about this, but nothing to do with what you went through this year."

Her words were so clear and confident, the doubt that had started to worm its way into his brain dissipated immediately. He took a breath and tried to get his body back under his control. He eased his hold on her, though it took an enormous amount of discipline, and took a half step back. He needed the distance, but he couldn't bring himself to stop touching her, so he left his hand resting on her low back. He underestimated just how much he'd want to slide his hand over the curve of her luscious bottom and had to take several slow breaths to maintain control.

Vivi's eyes had fallen, but she lifted them again. Her gaze was clear and direct. "How long is too damn long?" she asked.

He thought for a moment. "Well, there are two answers to that. There's the one where I tell you maybe I thought about kissing you back when you were still in high school." When her eyes widened, he couldn't help the smile that curled the corner of his mouth. "There's the other one where I tell you I thought about more than that this last year or so. I haven't really been in a place to do anything about it until now."

His chest tightened at what his own words meant. When he heard them aloud, they held a potency he hadn't contemplated.

Vivi was quiet for several beats, a flush staining her cheeks. One of her hands fell from his chest. She started fiddling with the silver charm bracelet on her wrist. She took a gulp of air before she spoke. "Okay then. That clears it up."

"How about you?"

Another few beats passed, and she took another deep breath. "Okay, you were honest, so I'll be honest. I suppose I have two answers as well. The first is I might have had more than a few times when I thought about kissing you back in high school. The second is life happened and then…" She paused, the soft clink of the charms on her bracelet audible as she looked up at him. "You came home again…and I've thought about it a lot more since then."

What he wanted to do was lift her in his arms and find the first place he could to bury himself inside of her, but he wasn't after quick satisfaction. Not with Vivi. He wanted the time to see what lay between them and if it meant as much as he suspected. If his cat had anything to say about it, he wouldn't be waiting at all. Alas, human reason managed to filter through. So, he shackled his impulses and slowly eased his hand off her waist.

"Are you walking home?" he asked.

At her nod, he continued. "I'll walk with you."

They walked through the quiet night. At some point along the way, he reached for her hand. When they walked up the steps to her house, he looked down and allowed himself one small moment. He dipped his head and caught her lips in a quick kiss. Just that, and it took all of his willpower to pull back.

After she closed the door and locked it behind him, he walked down the stairs and returned to where he'd left his car. His lion simmered, the shackling of his desire went against every grain of the lion side of his shifter self. The chilly, quiet night settled him and by the time he made it to his car, the heat inside had begun to abate.

Chapter 2

Vivi held a toothbrush in one hand, vigorously scrubbing her teeth while she clipped her hair back in a barrette with the other hand. She ran the faucet and rinsed her mouth. Just as she turned the water off, a loud thump came from the kitchen.

"Julianna!" she called out, snatching a towel and drying her hands as she raced down the hallway.

Julianna looked up, her dark brown eyes wide. A milk carton lay on its side with milk spreading in a pool by Julianna's feet. Julianna glanced up with a grimace. "Sorry, Mom."

A blur of black and white caught Vivi's eyes. Jax, Julianna's beloved young cat, dashed across the kitchen and skidded into the puddle of milk. Impatience rose inside Vivi. Every morning felt like a race. Small accidents like this only added to the hurry. Vivi strode quickly to Jax's side and promptly dropped the towel in her hands on the milk. "Sorry Jax. No time to let you try to clean this up." Jax sat on his haunches and set to cleaning his wet paws, unperturbed.

"Mom! That's a bathroom towel!"

Vivi shrugged. "So what?" She brushed Julianna's brown hair out of her eyes and dropped a kiss on her forehead. When she looked back at the floor, the towel had already absorbed the milk. "See, it's all gone," she said as she picked up the towel and carried it to the sink to wring it out. "Pick up the milk carton please."

Julianna immediately picked it up and started to carry it to the trash. "Hey, give me that," Vivi said, turning and holding her hand out.

Julianna looked up, her eyes confused.

"Hey, if there's any milk left in there, we can still drink it," Vivi said with a grin.

Julianna smiled doubtfully, but she carried the carton over and handed it to her mother. Vivi shook it, feeling almost nothing swishing back and forth in the bottom. "Oh well, it was worth checking." She handed it back to Julianna who quickly dropped it in the trash before she slid into a chair at the kitchen table.

Vivi opened the fridge, hoping she'd find an extra carton of milk, so Julianna could have her cereal, and she could have a dash of milk in her coffee. No such luck. She tended to live day to day when it came to shopping and anything that cost money. She wouldn't trade her life for anything, but being a single mother meant money was tight all the time. When she got pregnant with Julianna, her landscaping business had been in full swing. It was a small business, but it paid the bills and she loved it. Once she had Julianna, she quickly realized her money didn't stretch as far. Her business kept her afloat and a few shifts a week at Quinn's filled the gaps.

Back before Julianna came along, she'd fancied herself in love with Chris Barnett, a shifter who she'd met when he spent a summer in Painter. Chris had been fun and showered her with attention, up until the day she told him about her unexpected pregnancy. Before she'd even had a chance to consider what she wanted to do, he made it clear he expected her to *not* have the baby. He'd also turned cold and distant.

To this day, she didn't know if her choice to have Julianna had been spurred by his arrogant assumption she wouldn't have her. It didn't matter because Vivi loved Julianna to pieces and wouldn't have changed the course of events even if she could've. It would have been nice for Julianna to have a father who was a part of her life, but if Vivi had learned one thing, it was that learning to be at peace with circumstances beyond her control made life a lot easier.

For now, she grabbed a yogurt and a banana. Moments later, she set the bowl down in front of Julianna. "Maple yogurt with bananas!" she announced with a mock bow. "Breakfast of the champions."

Julianna giggled and immediately lifted her spoon to start eating. A while later, Vivi watched the bus drive away, bright yellow in the misty gray rain of the morning. She sat down at the kitchen table with a sigh. By some small miracle, there were only a few dishes piled up by the sink. Her eyes traveled around the kitchen. Her house was a small bungalow, like many of the homes in her neighborhood. The kitchen had counters with cabinets above lining two walls with the refrigerator tucked into a corner. The sink was situated in the center of one wall and a stove on the other. There was just enough room for a small round table by the archway that led into the living room. On a clear day, the windows let sun in that streamed all the way into the kitchen. With today being rainy, the light was dim inside.

She pushed her chair back and strode into the living

room. The mountains loomed in the distance, partially obscured by the clouds. Painter was nestled high in the mountains of Colorado. Vivi loved it here. The shifter side of her only felt at home in the mountains and skirting the edge of wilderness. She loved where her house was because she could see the mountains everyday, her best friend lived a few houses down the street, and downtown Painter was within walking distance.

Her eyes landed on one of the ferns hanging in the window. She quickly snagged the watering can off the table by the wall and filled it. After she watered her plants, she tossed her raincoat on and grabbed her purse before heading out the door. She jogged down the porch stairs and stopped by her car, considering for a second whether to drive. She quickly decided against it and headed for a walk through the drizzle.

As she turned onto Main Street and saw the bright red lettering for Mile High Grounds, her favorite coffee shop, which happened to be owned by her best friend, Heath strolled through her thoughts for the hundredth time since last night's unexpected kiss. She found herself constantly batting the thoughts away—it was almost too much to think about what happened. There was a good chance she might run into him at Mile High. He was there as often as she was, seeing as Sophia was his sister. Just thinking about him sent flutters twirling through her belly. She could hardly believe their kiss had even happened. Normally she'd have called Sophia to babble about something like that, but she couldn't. Not now. She'd successfully hidden her crush on Heath from Sophia way back when they were in high school together. While he'd been away in the military, she'd simply let it go. Chris had come along and sort of swept her off her feet. After that blew up, she was too busy being a mother to think of anything remotely resembling romance.

Then, Heath came home. His first year home had been a doozy. Between his car accident, grueling recovery, falling into the trap of painkiller addiction and then brushing up against the shifter smuggling network, he'd had more than his share of troubles. Through it all, Vivi had fought against the tide of feeling welling up for him. She reached Mile High Grounds and pushed through the swinging door. The scent of coffee filled the small space. It was mid-morning and the coffee shop was in full swing. The tables were full and a line of customers waited by the counter. She glanced around and breathed a silent sigh of relief to find Heath wasn't there. Her relief was immediately followed by a twinge of disappointment. She wanted to see him again, but she didn't want to see him again. The silly, hopeful side of herself wanted to see if sparks flew again when she saw him. While her rational brain reminded her she couldn't get all romantic and hopeful. Too many complications. With a shake of her head to knock Heath out of her thoughts, she went to stand in line by the counter.

***

Heath swung his truck into a parking spot on Main Street. As he walked across the street, he turned around quickly, realizing he'd forgotten to lock it. He hit the button on his remote key and paused where he stood. The truck he drove now was shiny and black. It was similar to the one he'd had for years, albeit quite a few years younger. That truck had been totaled when he'd slid off the icy highway that cold night over a year ago. That truck had felt like an old friend because it had sat waiting for him after years away in the military. This one was too shiny, too new. He took a breath and savored the sharpness of his thoughts.

After a year of living in the fog of pain and painkillers, he appreciated every moment he could think clearly. He'd had a good six months of clarity and was still grateful for every second. Turning on his heel, he strode down the sidewalk and pushed through the door of Mile High Grounds. Sophia had opened this coffee shop while he was away and it had become the hottest spot in town for coffee. He was damn proud of his sister.

He took a few steps into the café and awareness prickled over his skin. He lifted his head to find Vivi standing by the counter. With her hip leaned against it, she gestured with her hand as she spoke to Sophia. Sophia's dark hair was pulled back on one side with a barrette. She wore charcoal gray leggings with a stretchy black mini skirt over them. Her navy raincoat hung over her shoulders. A bolt of heat shot through him, and his body tightened merely at the sight of her. He was going to have to play this cool. He might have let desire get ahead of him the other night, but he had enough sense to know he had to proceed carefully.

Vivi couldn't just be a fling. Aside from the fact that she was Sophia's best friend and Sophia would kill him if he treated Vivi with anything but the utmost respect, she meant too much to him. For now, he yanked on the reins of his control and walked slowly up to the counter. Tommy Dawson, one of Sophia's employees, saw him first. "Hey man, what'll it be today?" Tommy asked, his brown eyes crinkling at the corners with his smile.

"I'll take straight coffee today."

At Heath's reply, Vivi turned, her blue eyes slamming into his. He nodded in her direction. Sophia glanced his way as well. "Hey Heath! No mocha today?"

Heath shrugged. "They're good, but I'm not in the mood for anything sweet right now. Straight black coffee is what I need."

"Coming right up," Tommy said before he stepped back from the counter to get the coffee in question.

Heath found his eyes wandering to Vivi. Her jacket was unzipped, revealing the snug white t-shirt she wore. She had a penchant for those fitted cotton shirts, which drove him half out of his mind. The shirt pulled tight across her full breasts and traced the dip at her waist. Lust jolted through him, and he tore his eyes away from her. They landed on Tommy who was returning to the counter, coffee in hand. Tommy's eyes bounced from Vivi to Heath, a glimmer of speculation in them. He slid the coffee across the counter to Heath.

Heath grabbed it and took a gulp. He tugged his wallet out and tossed a five-dollar bill on the counter. Before Sophia had a chance to say anything, he spoke up. "If you won't ring me up, put it in the tip jar."

Tommy chuckled and swiped the bill, stuffing it in the tip jar. "She won't ring you up."

Sophia's mock glare flicked between them. "I get to let family have coffee on the house if I want!"

Heath shrugged. "Either way is fine with me. Coffee's excellent." He took another gulp and chanced a look in Vivi's direction again. She'd turned away and was asking Sophia something.

"Did Daniel hear anything else from Roger after they searched those properties in Wyoming?"

Heath stepped closer, moving out of the way of a customer who approached the counter. A subtle hint of lavender drifted to him. The scent reminded him of how Vivi felt close against him the other night. It had only lasted mere minutes, but he'd replayed it over and over on a loop in his brain. He took another swallow of coffee and focused his mind on the moment.

"Any news from Roger?" he asked, referencing Vivi's question. Roger was a local police officer in Painter and one of the shifters helping lead the investigation into the shifter drug smuggling network. Last fall had brought a big break in the years-long investigation when the ringleader had been uncovered. Nelson Weaver was on the lam and the police were systematically searching massive tracts of land owned by Daniel Hayes. Daniel happened to be Nelson's long-lost nephew who'd returned to Painter and swept Sophia off her feet.

Nelson had been using his family's old logging properties as waypoints and storage locations for the smuggling network. Mountain lion shifters were sadly ideal to smuggle drugs because they could cover a lot of ground and no one would ever suspect them. Nelson had turned sour and bitter after the death of his other nephew, Daniel's brother. That death echoed through Painter because it had put shifters at risk. Daniel's brother, at the young age of ten, had shifted in a public park and been shot. His family fled Painter under a cloud of pain and shame. Nelson turned to drink and drugs and somewhere along the way decided he could make good money by organizing shifters to smuggle drugs.

Aside from the obvious reasons any community would want to put a stop to drug smuggling, Painter had held the secret existence of shifters close for centuries. With shifters involved in drug smuggling, the entire community was at risk. Any involvement in illegal activities shook the foundation of shifter secrecy. Painter was one of many shifter communities and sadly, the shifter smuggling network had spread its tentacles all the way across the country. Other areas had successfully quashed it, but it had been like chasing ghosts in Painter. Only when they discovered Nelson's role and how he'd used his family's logging properties, which were spread far and wide in the West and into the edges of the Midwest, did the shifter community finally feel like they had a chance to wipe the network out. Nelson had disappeared after a fight in the woods a few months ago.

Sophia looked toward Heath with a shrug. "Not much. Daniel said all Roger had to offer was they'd searched several more areas and turned up no sign of Nelson. They've found more storage locations on almost every property and torn them down. Problem is those old logging properties are massive. They're fanning out, but if they want to truly cover every inch, they need to use air support. That would draw attention we don't want."

"Yeah, it's not like we can say we're searching for a mountain lion and a man. If he's in the woods and moving, he's most likely in lion form," Heath added. He shook his head and sighed, leaning his hip against the counter. "They will find him. It's just matter of how long it takes. No matter what, Nelson can only dodge for so long. I stopped by to see Roger last week, and he mentioned they've alerted the police in every shifter community. There's no way for him to hide out too long anywhere."

Vivi finally looked over at Heath. She twisted the elastic cord on her raincoat around her index finger. "I keep trying to remember that. I'm just worried they'll eventually stop looking."

"Vivi, they're not going to stop looking," Sophia said with a shake of her head.

"Maybe, maybe not. It's already been a few months since Nelson took off and everyone's getting complacent. I hear all the gossip at Quinn's. Not many shifters are worried about it anymore."

"The police are committed, so I'm pretty sure they'll keep looking. If they don't, we will," Heath said.

Vivi's blue eyes swung to his. She held his gaze for a long moment before she released the elastic cord she'd wound tightly around her finger. "Right," she said softly.

Chapter 3

A few days later, Vivi carefully set the peony plant in the hole she'd prepared in the flowerbed. After sifting soil over it, she added mulch and watered it. She stood up and knocked the loose soil off of her work gloves. After taking a step back, she surveyed the work she'd done. She'd mulched and planted flowerbeds surrounding the house. These were her favorite jobs because she loved flowers and enjoyed when customers gave her free rein to be artistic with them. It would be another year or two before the flowers would settle and show enough growth to fill the area.

She turned away and gathered her tools, setting them in the wheelbarrow. A while later, she walked up the stairs to her back porch and plunked down in a chair by a small round table. She spent a lot of time out here when the weather was nice. The porch looked out over her backyard, which bloomed throughout the summer in staggered phases. She kicked off her dusty boots and stretched her legs. Jax leapt up onto the railing and walked across to the table beside Vivi.

"Hey Jax!" She held out her hand, and Jax promptly rubbed his head against it, his purr a loud rumble.

At the sound of a squirrel scurrying up a tree nearby, Jax lifted his head. Vivi stood. "Wishful thinking," she commented to Jax.

She brushed past him, stroking her hand over his back, and headed straight for a hot shower. When she walked back through the living room into the kitchen, rubbing her hair with a towel, she heard the sound of a car pulling up in her driveway. She walked to the window and looked outside. Heath was climbing out of his black truck. Her heart stuttered and then lunged forward. Heat raced through her. Somehow, she didn't quite know how, she'd been managing to keep thoughts of their kiss at bay. It was almost too much to think about. Every time her thoughts bumped against the memory, she shied away.

She wondered why he was here, but she didn't have much time to obsess about it. He jogged up the steps to the back porch. She met him at the door where Jax was twining himself around Heath's ankles. His eyes crinkled at the corners with a slow smile when she opened the screen door. "I don't recall you having a cat."

"That's Jax. Julianna found him at the park wandering around crying when he was a kitten. She carried him home in her backpack." Vivi shrugged. "That was six months ago. He's still a kitten really."

Heath glanced down at Jax who was batting at the end of the shoelace on Heath's boot. His low chuckle sent a shiver up her spine. "Right." His green gaze caught hers. "Can I come in?"

Her breath was shallow as she nodded. She tried to shove away the questions shouting in her mind. *Why is he here? What does he want?* She was a silly muddled mess, and all over him simply stopping by her house. Several beats passed. Heath angled his head to the side. "So, uh, should I go?"

"Oh. Oh no! Come on in," she said, her words rapid and jerky. She stepped back from the door and held it open. Jax dashed inside. Heath followed at a more leisurely pace. Vivi let the door fall closed and stepped over to the counter. She'd known Heath for her entire life, yet she had no idea how to act right now. He'd been to her house many times, although usually with Sophia. In fact, she couldn't think of a single time he'd stopped by on his own. She curled her hands around the edge of the counter and looked over at him.

He stood by the kitchen table. Jax was standing on the chair by his hip, rubbing his head against Heath's hand. As usual, Jax's purr was audible throughout the room. Heath looked up. The corner of his mouth lifted in a smile. "He's got a helluva a purr."

His comment eased the tension knotting inside of her, and a soft laugh escaped. "He sure does. He sleeps with Julianna, and he purrs so loud, I can't believe she sleeps through it."

"How's Julianna?"

"She's good. She likes her new teacher this year, which is a relief because she didn't do too well with her first grade teacher."

"No? She's so easy going. Hard to imagine that."

"She's easy going, but she's got a stubborn streak. That ran right into a teacher who didn't have much patience with Julianna. I was busy running interference between her and the school. Last year was a learning experience for both of us. She got through first grade, and I learned how to argue with the school." Vivi shook her head with a rueful grin. "I thought I was done with school when I graduated. Nobody tells you it starts all over once you have your own kid."

Heath grinned. "You never did mind kicking up a fuss. You're an amazing mother. You'll handle it just fine, no matter what comes Julianna's way."

She flushed and looked away from his eyes. "I do my best, but it's harder than I ever guessed." She managed a breath and lifted her gaze again.

"I bet it is." His grin faded, and his voice was gruff. He stroked Jax once more and took three long strides across the room to stop a few feet in front of her.

Her heart gave a hard kick, and her breath hitched in her throat. He wore a gray cotton jersey shirt with the fabric faded and soft, hugging his muscled chest and abs. A decade in the Marine Special Forces had honed his body. Even after a year that had left him physically battered after his car accident, he still emanated pure strength and masculinity. Now it was tempered and hardened from what he'd been through. She knew he'd fought plenty of battles during his time in the military, but she thought the personal battle he'd endured this past year had honed him physically and mentally in a way nothing ever had before.

He cleared his throat. "So, uh, we haven't had a chance to talk again since the other night."

Somehow, she didn't quite know how, she managed to nod even though her pulse was galloping along and she could barely get a full breath of air. After several taut seconds ticked by, Heath cleared his throat again. She could feel the heat crawl up her neck and into her cheeks.

She dredged up her words. "I, uh, don't really know what to say." She was instantly annoyed with herself. He'd always flustered her, but before he'd kissed her, she'd managed to hold herself together. She liked to think of herself as a strong woman, one who didn't fall apart inside just because of a man. But Heath had this strange effect on her where she felt vulnerable and strong at once, tossed and turned in the tide of wishes, dreams, hopes…and pure lust.

Heath nodded, his eyes locked on her. He remained still for several long seconds before he moved decisively. In one step, he was suddenly a whisper away from her. He lifted a hand and brushed a damp curl away from her face, tucking it behind her ear. Her skin prickled in the wake of his touch. He angled his head, his eyes darkening. He appeared to be giving her the chance to say something. The air grew thick with desire. Barely able to hear over the thundering of her heart with her belly clenching, she waited. He fit his mouth over hers. A shock of pleasure scored her the second his lips met hers. He traced her lips with his tongue before he swept inside at her gasp. His tongue stroked against hers, while he slid a hand into her hair, cupping the nape of her neck and angling her head to the side.

By the time his lips left hers, she was breathless and wild inside. He trailed wet kisses down along the column of her throat. Want lashed at her, and she arched into him, savoring the hard, heated length of him against her hips. He growled against her skin when she rocked her hips into him. Her channel throbbed and moisture drenched her. He kept trailing his lips down, into the dip where her neck met her shoulder. Her skin was soft and so sensitive, she couldn't hold back the low moan that escaped when he lightly bit there.

His hand traveled down, an electric path of heat along her spine, and cupped her bottom. He groaned against her skin. After she'd showered, she'd tossed on a thin cotton shirt with a few buttons between her breasts. His lips made their way into the valley there. With a rough tug with his free hand, the buttons popped free. Her nipples were tight, straining against the thin fabric. He didn't hesitate and tugged the shirt down to expose one breast. He lifted his head, just slightly. She dragged her eyes open to find his waiting—hot and dark. For a flash, she felt so exposed and bare. All of the longing she'd hidden was there for him to see because she couldn't hide it right now.

He shook his head, so subtly it was almost imperceptible. "Don't," he whispered. The question in her eyes must have shown. "Don't doubt this," he added, his voice rough.

He dipped his head again, just as his palm curled under her breast. He dragged his thumb back and forth across her nipple, so taut it nearly ached. She could barely hold herself upright, wracked with sensation swirling inside. His strong arm was wrapped around her with his palm still cupping her bottom and holding her against him. Without his strength to hold her, her knees would have buckled when his lips closed over her nipple. He swirled his tongue around her nipple and drew it into his mouth. She arched into him, her breath coming in shallow pants. In a distant corner of her mind, she heard the sound of the school bus stopping outside, the brakes giving off a low-pitched squeal. She ignored it and dragged her hands down Heath's back, savoring the flex of his muscles under her palms.

The sound of feet running down the driveway nudged her consciousness. Heath tore his lips from her breast and immediately tugged her shirt back into place, swiftly buttoning the few buttons. Her thoughts were fuzzed with desire, and she had to shake her head sharply to pull herself together. Julianna was running up the back steps now.

"Oh God," Vivi said, hastily straightening her shirt and running a hand through her mussed hair.

She looked over at Heath as he stepped back,

creating space between them. Cool air drifted over her skin, soothing the heat inside. She was momentarily stunned. She heard Julianna talking to Jax. He must have pushed through the screen door onto the porch. The moment gave Vivi enough time to gather the remnants of her control. She gulped in air and glanced up at Heath. Before she had a chance to say anything, the screen door swung open and Julianna came through. Heath took another step back, smoothly turning and leaning his hips against the counter.

"Hey Mom!" Julianna said as she left her backpack by the door and ran to wrap her arms around Vivi's waist. Julianna barely stopped moving as she dropped her arms and stepped to the refrigerator to pull it open. She grabbed a juice box and turned, only then appearing to notice Heath who was quietly waiting.

"Heath!" Julianna leapt from where she stood and flung herself against him. "I didn't know you were coming over," she said as she stepped away and looked up at him.

Heath gave her braid an affectionate tug. "I stopped by to say hi to your mom and now I get the bonus of seeing you."

Vivi considered that he'd done a lot more than say hi. She watched while Julianna picked up her juice box and speared it with the attached straw. She chattered with Heath, twirling her braid in one hand and sipping her juice with the other. Vivi's heart tightened. Heath had been away for much of Julianna's first seven years, but Julianna had always thought of him like family. In the year or so since he'd been home, he'd been around enough for Julianna's attachment to him to deepen.

Vivi couldn't help but wonder what it would be like for Heath to be a father to Julianna. She instantly shoved that silly, wishful thought out of her mind. She could *not* go there. Vivi didn't need to create fantasies about what it would be like for Julianna to have a father who cared because then she'd want Heath even more than she already did. Julianna technically had a father. He just didn't happen to be around—at all. For all intents and purposes, Chris was nothing more than a sperm donor. Vivi tried to remember the last time she heard from Chris. In the first few years after Julianna was born, he called here and there and stopped by once in a while. Not once had he held Julianna when she was a baby. He moved on from Painter after that, and she hadn't heard from him since. Chris had been a charismatic whirlwind for her. He'd swept into town, new and different. Back then, she'd been working to the bone trying to get her landscaping business going and wondering if she'd ever meet anyone who made her feel alive the way Heath did.

With Chris, it was all on the surface, but only hindsight had given her that perspective. Once something real happened, such as her pregnancy, the shiny surface of their relationship dulled quickly. Chris liked things to be fun, light and easy. He also lived and breathed the belief that shifters required freedom. Commitment and parenting were like shackles to him. She suspected he'd had a few brush ups with the law, but she never knew. She didn't like thinking about it, but he had partied here and there with Nelson Weaver. When she first heard the faint rumors about shifters smuggling drugs, she immediately thought of Chris. He would have liked the thrill and the easy money. Even now, she hadn't dredged up the courage to mention this to Sophia. She figured if he was involved, they'd eventually find out. Or maybe not. All she cared about was driving the network out of Painter. She'd seen it cause too much pain.

She shook her head, nudging her thoughts off of Chris. Julianna snagged a banana off the counter. She looked up at Heath. "Are you staying for dinner? Mom's making crunchy macaroni and cheese."

Heath's eyes swung from Julianna to Vivi, crinkling at the corners with his smile. He arched a brow. Vivi shrugged. She'd love for him to stay for dinner, but she was half terrified because she didn't know what this was for them. Before they'd kissed and now kissed again, she'd have easily said yes. She might have had to hold the whispers of her desire at bay, but Heath was like family. Befuddled and tossed asunder by the avalanche of feelings Heath elicited, she didn't want Julianna to think anything was amiss. If she said no, Julianna would wonder why. Heath's eyes were still on her while Julianna looked at them expectantly. Vivi nodded, and Heath looked back to Julianna. "I'd love to stay for dinner. How about you tell me what crunchy macaroni and cheese is?"

After a bite of her banana, Julianna explained. "Mom makes it on a pan, so the cheese gets all crusty. I like it when the cheese gets a little burned, so Mom started making it like that. Do you like burned cheese?"

Vivi bit back a laugh at Julianna's question. Heath simply nodded, his expression completely somber. "I do like burned cheese. Your mom's really smart to come up with that. Sounds like it's crunchy all through and not just in the corners."

Julianna nodded enthusiastically, a wide smile spreading across her face. "It is! It's the best. Almost all the cheese gets crunchy!" She finished her banana and stood up to put the peel in the stainless steel compost bucket under the sink. After she carefully put the lid over it, she whirled around. "Mom, can I go outside for a little bit?"

"Of course. If you ride your bike, you know the rules. Wear your helmet and stay off Main Street. Be back in an hour, okay?"

Julianna nodded quickly. "Yup!" At that, she dashed past them. The screen door slammed behind her. Vivi could see her grab her bike helmet before she ran down the porch stairs. Out of reflex, Vivi walked through the archway into the living room and watched while Julianna wheeled her bike down the driveway and climbed on. She'd been riding a bike since she was four years old. In the last year or so, she'd moved past training wheels and prided herself on being able to ride on her own. Vivi loved living in Painter for many reasons, including the fact it was a safe community. Neighbors watched out for each other. Vivi knew most of their neighbors and felt safe having Julianna explore nearby. Only in the last few years had she had a few inklings of worry with the shifter smuggling network popping up. She knew those shifters involved relied on staying hidden, but her worry stemmed from what it meant to have shifters like that among them. Since multiple arrests had occurred over the last six months or so and Nelson had taken off, things had settled down significantly.

She felt Heath come to her side. His energy was so potent, it was impossible for her to ignore. She took a slow breath, keeping her eyes on Julianna as she peddled down the street. Her purple helmet was a bobbing bright spot as she made her way down the road.

"You sure you don't mind me staying for dinner?" Heath asked, his voice gruff.

Vivi slipped her hands in the pockets of her jeans, her eyes canting down to the floor. The hardwood floor was scuffed from many years of use. She traced one of the boards with her bare toes. "Of course I don't mind. I, uh, I'd like it if you stayed." She glanced up and caught his eyes. "Julianna will love it. She loves company, and she thinks of you like family. Plus, it sounds like you like burnt cheese as much as she does," she offered with a soft laugh.

She turned away and busied herself at the sink as her belly fluttered and heat slid through her veins.

Chapter 4

Heath climbed down, the stainless steel ladder flexing with each step. He paused to adjust his tool belt. When he reached the bottom, he tossed the small bag he carried onto the ground. He was at Daniel's old farmhouse helping to repair the roof. Daniel was hoping to get the farmhouse in good enough shape for he and Sophia to move here soon. Heath stepped off the ladder and headed over to the other side of the house where Daniel was working.

"Roof's good to go now," Heath called up to Daniel.

Daniel stood on a ladder and was busy refitting a window on the second floor. He finished drilling and reached through the open window to set the power drill down before glancing over his shoulder. "All done here. Give me a sec." He climbed down and strode across the lawn to Heath's side. "You think we took care of all the roof leaks?"

Heath nodded. "Yup. Took care of the last section today. You'll be good to go for another five years or more before you need to replace the roof. My best guess is your grandparents had the shingles replaced about fifteen years ago. If Nelson hadn't let this place go to shit, you might get a few more good years. Patches aren't as good as taking care of the whole thing."

Daniel shrugged. "They'll work for now." His blue eyes scanned the back of the sprawling farmhouse. "With your help, I'll have this place ready for winter. You think Sophia will be okay moving out here?"

Heath glanced to Daniel and considered how the moment he'd seen Daniel, he'd known Daniel was the man for his sister. Daniel was tall and dark with a quiet, reserved edge. Heath caught his eyes. "Soph will love it here. What's got you worried she won't?"

"She loves her little house. It's right down the street from Vivi, and she can walk to Mile High. It's not too far out of town here, but she won't be walking to work."

"Soph can appreciate what she's got now and appreciate what she'll have out here. You've been to our parents' house. We grew up in a place a lot like this. Soph loves being right by the wilderness. She can't shut up about the yard and her garden planning for this place. Relax. All she wants is to be with you."

Daniel held his eyes for a moment and nodded firmly. "I'll stop worrying. This whole thing is pretty new to me."

Heath chuckled. "No worries. Take my word for it though. Soph loves you."

At that, Heath turned and headed back to the front of the house. "Gonna grab my tools and head out. I need to stop by the bank before it closes today."

Daniel followed him around to the front of the farmhouse and paused by Heath's truck. "Thanks again for offering to help with all these repairs. There's no way I could've gotten this much work done on my own."

"No need to thank me. Anytime you need help, say the word. You're family."

Heath started his truck and put it in gear to back out. He glanced back to Daniel. "I can come back out tomorrow afternoon if you want help with the rest of the windows." Daniel was slowly replacing all the old, single pane windows with new insulated windows. Old farmhouses like this were heat sinks without those updates and others.

"That'd be great. Only if you have the time though."

"Wouldn't offer unless I did."

At that, Heath backed up and headed to town. On the short drive, he considered why he had so much time to help Daniel. A year and a half ago, he'd been a decorated Marine. He supposed he still was, although it was hard to remember what it felt like to feel worthy of that. He'd gone straight into the Marines after high school. He couldn't quite recall what his plan had been, but once he got started, he rapidly climbed the ladder of promotions and ended up on track for training in the Special Forces. He'd thrived during his five years in the Special Forces. He liked the commitment and functioned well under pressure. A year and a half ago, he'd come home for a long leave over the holidays. His life went into a tailspin after the car accident. To this day, he was relieved he'd applied for an honorable discharge once he realized how long his recovery would take. He couldn't have known he'd spiral into a fog of pain and addiction.

Now that he was putting his life back together, he had to figure out what he meant to do. Thus far, he'd been doing what came easily—pick up construction jobs here and there. He'd always loved building because working with his hands kept him focused and he enjoyed the sense of completion when a project was done. He had enough money saved to get by for another little while, but he was formulating a plan to do more than odd jobs. He had a meeting today to set up a business loan to start his own construction company.

Once he turned onto Main Street, he swung into the parking lot at the bank. Mile High Grounds was across the street. He glanced over while he walked to the bank entrance. He saw the swing of Vivi's long dark hair as she pushed through the door. His body tightened. *Holy hell.* All he had to do was see her—from across the street for crying out loud—and it was like a switch flipped on inside of him.

***

Vivi sipped on her coffee while she entered numbers into her monthly accounting system. She had an accountant who helped her with taxes, but she managed the monthly billing on her own. She was spending the late afternoon at Mile High Grounds, her preferred place for working on this part of her business. When she reached the last row, she clicked the icon for the number to calculate. She'd see whether her monthly payments balanced out with her expenses and left enough to cover the bills. After a few seconds, she breathed a sigh of relief. She'd have more than enough to cover her bills this month and some to set aside for winter expenses.

"Hey there," Sophia said as she slid into the chair across from Vivi with a mug of coffee in hand. "Tommy's prepping a sandwich for you. How's the accounting going?"

Vivi hit the save button and glanced up at Sophia. Sophia shared Heath's almost black hair and green eyes. Sophia had been Vivi's best friend for as long as she could remember. They'd both been born and raised in Painter and had attended pre-school together.

"It's done and the numbers look good. Enough to get me through the month." Vivi paused for another swallow of coffee. "How'd you guess I was starving?"

Sophia grinned. "Because you usually don't bother with lunch. I told Tommy to make you the red pepper and hummus sandwich."

Vivi's stomach growled, prompting a giggle from Sophia. "Clearly, I need to eat," Vivi said with a wry grin. She closed up the accounting program and tucked her laptop away in its bag. "How are things going out at the farmhouse?"

"Busy, busy. Daniel's out there everyday. He wants to have everything ready for us to move in before winter." Sophia traced the edge of her coffee mug and chewed her lip. "I'm going to miss living a few houses down the street from you," she said softly.

Vivi angled her head to the side. "Hey, don't tell me you're worrying about that. You'll be a ten minute drive away."

Sophia took a gulp of coffee and leaned back in her chair. "I know it's only ten minutes, but…"

Vivi cut her off. "But nothing! Sure, it's great having you right down the street, but we'll see each other just as much. You're going to love that giant yard! I'll come help you plant flowers whenever you want."

Sophia held Vivi's gaze for a long moment. "I know, I know. I'm being silly."

"No you're not. I'll miss having you so close, but this is a good change. You and Daniel are going to love being out at the farmhouse."

Sophia took a breath, her shoulders relaxing when she let it out. "There are only two things I'll miss— stopping by your place on the way to work and walking to work. Other than that, I can't wait." A slow smile spread across her face.

Vivi lifted her coffee mug in toast. She felt a little ping in her chest. She was so happy Sophia found Daniel, but occasionally it illuminated what she didn't have in her life—namely a man who adored her and was beyond ready to dive into sharing their life together. She mentally shook her thoughts away. At that moment, Tommy approached the table with two plates.

"Sandwiches for both of you," he said, setting the plates down with a flourish. "Need anything else?"

Vivi glanced down at the generous sandwich on Sophia's fresh baked multigrain bread. She shook her head. "Nope. This is perfect."

Tommy leaned against the wall by their table. "I was telling Soph that we'd organize a moving crew for her. You in?" he asked, his warm brown eyes on Vivi.

"Of course! But you'd better make sure to round up lots of your young guy friends. I'm a hard worker, but I'm not tall and strong like you."

Tommy chuckled. "Already on it. I told the guys from my basketball pick up games we'd give 'em food and coffee for the day. They're all in."

The bell jingled over the door, and Tommy pushed away from the wall. "Holler if you need anything else."

Sophia waved him off. "Don't worry about us. Thanks Tommy!"

Vivi dug into her sandwich. After a few minutes, she glanced down at her almost empty plate and sighed. "Oh man, that was so good."

Sophia finished chewing the last bite of her sandwich. "I'll vouch for Tommy's sandwiches, but everything tastes better when you're starving." She pushed back her chair and held her hand out for Vivi's plate. "I'll get us some fresh coffee. Want a pastry for dessert?"

Vivi handed over her plate. "Definitely. How about you get that and I'll take care of the coffee?" She stood and snagged both of their empty coffee mugs.

Sophia shrugged and headed to the counter, slipping behind and disappearing into the back room. Vivi followed her and paused in front of the counter. Tommy glanced over. "Refills?" he asked.

At her nod, he reached for the two coffee mugs and quickly filled them from the house coffee pot. "Hang on, let me add espresso shots," he said as he stepped behind the espresso machine.

The bell jangled over the door again, and Vivi reflexively glanced over her shoulder to see Heath walking in. Awareness pinged in her center. She couldn't keep her eyes off of him as he walked through the coffee shop. He wore a battered denim jacket and faded jeans with brown leather work boots. He pulled his sunglasses off and tucked them in his jacket pocket. Vivi's breath hitched when his eyes caught hers. Her mind spun back to the other night when he'd stayed for dinner. He'd been a model dinner guest. The standards were different when it came to dinner with an enthusiastic seven year old whose curiosity was never ending. He'd been patient and gracious with Julianna's endless questions through dinner and helped with clean up afterwards. Vivi's body had hummed the entire time. It was the kind of evening she wished she could have more often. Not just the part where Heath's mere presence made her body spin like a top, but the part where she wasn't quite so alone in her little world, where someone else was there for the mundane parts of life.

When it came time for him to go, she'd walked him to the door and he'd slayed her with another one of his kisses. Kisses she was coming to consider a risk to her very being because not only did they send her body into a tailspin of longing, but they made her heart hope for things she didn't know if she could ever have with Heath.

For a few seconds, Vivi forgot where they were. Locked in Heath's green gaze, flutters amassed in her belly.

"Here you go," Tommy said, his voice cutting through her daze.

The sound of the coffee mugs sliding across the counter nudged her a little further into awareness. She tore her eyes from Heath and turned back to the counter. She wrapped her hands around the mugs and lifted her eyes to find Tommy watching her with a barely perceptible grin. "What?" she asked.

His eyes glanced past her shoulder where she knew Heath was approaching. "If you were hoping no one would notice, you might as well forget that," he said, his grin expanding.

She could feel the heat spread up her neck and battled to gather her composure. With a gulp of air, she shook her head sharply and glared at Tommy who only chuckled in return. She wished she wasn't so obvious, but Heath brought everything inside of her right to the surface.

Heath reached the counter. "Hey there, how's it going?" he asked generally, his eyes bouncing between her and Tommy.

Before Vivi had a chance to reply, Sophia pushed through the swinging door from the back area with two plates in hand. "Hey Heath!"

Heath glanced her way. "Hey Soph. Came for a quick coffee."

"What'll it be?" Tommy asked.

"Shot in the dark. To go," Heath replied. "I've got a meeting over at the bank in a few."

"Got it." Tommy turned away and quickly prepped

Heath's coffee.

Vivi stood there, frozen in place, her hands curled around the two mugs of coffee. Sophia was asking Heath questions about the work on the farmhouse. Only a few minutes passed before Tommy handed over Heath's coffee and Heath turned to leave. Just before he walked away from the counter, his eyes caught hers. For a second, she thought he was going to say something, but he merely nodded. She watched him walk away, the longing to touch him so strong, she gripped the coffee mugs a little tighter.

Sophia's voice came over her shoulder. "I heated up two cinnamon rolls for us. I know it's not breakfast, but they're your favorite."

Vivi mentally shook herself and turned back from the door. "Cinnamon rolls are perfect, especially with coffee," she said, forcing her attention off of Heath and back to the moment at hand.

She followed Sophia back to their table in the corner. She nibbled on the cinnamon roll, which was near perfection—soft, flaky and buttery with the perfect balance of sugar and cinnamon. After several quiet moments, Sophia cleared her throat. Vivi whipped her gaze up to find Sophia watching her. Sophia knew her better than anyone. Vivi knew she'd notice something might be up. She shifted in her seat and took another bite of her cinnamon roll.

"Okay, I'll just ask. What's up with you and Heath?"

Tension knotted in Vivi's stomach. She didn't know how to reconcile her long-dormant feelings for Heath flaring to life and the fact she'd hidden them from her best friend. It was all just rather inconvenient Heath happened to be Sophia's brother. She grabbed her coffee and took a gulp. "What do you mean?"

Sophia gave her a long look and then rolled her

eyes. "Okay, fine. I was trying to give you a chance, but I'm not blind. The last few months, whenever I see you two near each other, it's kind of obvious there's a thing. I wasn't going to say anything, but now it's *waaaay* obvious. If you're worried you can't talk to me about it because he's my brother, well that's just dumb. I'm not some overprotective sister. If something happens, you can skip the details, but other than that…" she paused and shrugged "…you don't need to hide anything from me."

The knot of tension eased, and Vivi took a slow breath. "I wasn't trying to hide anything, not on purpose. I just didn't know how to talk to you about it, and I don't even know what's happening." She set her coffee down and ran a hand through her hair, sifting through the stands and twirling a lock around her finger.

Sophia reached across the table and squeezed Vivi's free hand. "How about you stop trying to have an answer right away?"

"But…"

Sophia shook her head. "Look, I know you, you're going to spin circles in your brain if you try to make answers happen right now. All I'll say is this: take it one day at a time. You can tell me whatever you want, but I know that look in your eyes. You're about to wind yourself up."

Vivi smiled ruefully. "I know. It's not like much has happened, so don't go making it more than it is. It's just…" Her heart squeezed, almost painfully, as she considered the place Heath occupied in her heart. So much for moving on from him all those years ago. It was only easy as long as he was nowhere nearby. She glanced over at Sophia who was grinning. "What's so funny?"

Sophia shrugged. "If you ask me, you and Heath would be perfect together. Plus, it's fun to see you get a little rattled."

"Hey, no fair!"

"Oh right. You had all kinds of advice about how I should relax and let myself believe in possibilities when I met Daniel. Why don't you take your own advice?"

The light mirth that had started to swirl inside dissipated. "Because it's Heath. Things could get pretty damn awkward if things don't work out. That's a big 'if' by the way. If anything is happening, if we try to do something about it. If, if, if."

What Vivi didn't say aloud was that she didn't know how to allow herself to believe in possibilities. It wasn't just her heart that she risked, but Julianna's. It was hard enough to remember almost every day that she'd been too blind to see Chris for who he was. She couldn't dare run the risk of hoping for Heath to be the father Julianna had never had. She'd flung her heart on the line for Chris to watch him carelessly discard it. He'd claimed his cat couldn't tolerate being tied down in any way to anyone. That belief wasn't uncommon among male shifters. While she'd never heard Heath declare it, she wasn't so sure she could let herself believe in possibilities when there was a damn good possibility she might set herself up for a replay of allowing herself to be vulnerable, only to discover it wasn't worth it.

Chapter 5

Heath set his toolbox inside the back of his truck before closing the cap. He leaned against the truck and waited for Daniel. They'd spent the last few hours replacing some of the windows on the upper floor of the farmhouse. Daniel was putting his tools away in the garage and then they were heading out to do some scouting on the far side of town. Heath glanced around the yard. Sophia had clearly been at work on the flowerbeds running along the edge of the wraparound porch as fresh mulch was evident and the lingering weeds were gone. Sunlight fell in bars through the trees, dusting the grass in gold. It was early afternoon and the air held the lingering warmth from a warm autumn day. Leaves fluttered to the ground when a gust blew through the valley.

Heath leaned his head against the truck and closed his eyes, savoring the quiet. His mind immediately conjured Vivi. He'd promised himself he'd try to go slow, but his lion had other thoughts on that. After dinner when Julianna went to bed, he'd had to keep a firm grip on the need racing through him. The only thing that held him back was the knowledge he couldn't blow this because Vivi was too important. The sound of gravel crunching brought his eyes open again.

Daniel stopped a few feet in front of Heath. "Ready?"

Heath pushed away from his truck. "Let's go. Ride with me?"

A few minutes later, he was driving along the winding highway through the mountains. "You're gonna have to tell me where to go," he commented to Daniel. "I've been out this way plenty, but I'm not familiar with your grandparents' old logging properties."

"Stay on the main road for a good ten miles. Once we cross the river, we'll have to keep an eye out for an old logging road. You're definitely more familiar with the area than me," Daniel said with a gruff chuckle.

Years ago, after Daniel's brother died and he and his parents moved out of town, his grandparents remained behind with his uncle, Nelson Weaver. They owned a large and profitable timber company. When it became clear to them that Nelson wasn't headed in a good direction, they tied up their land holdings in their will to go to Daniel. Nelson inherited money, enough to carry him through his life had he managed it, but he blew through it and turned to drug smuggling as a way to make quick money. He started the smuggling network by using his parents' old properties for storage and delivery stations. Logging lands tended to be empty unless they were in use. Nelson capitalized on that convenience, along with the secrecy and the ease of travel for mountain lion shifters. He also took advantage of the fact that Daniel had been entirely unaware of his inheritance for years until he finally returned to Painter to find out about his family. The lands Daniel now owned were spread throughout Colorado into other Western states and into the Midwest. Colorado's problems with the smuggling network had lingered and now they knew why. With Nelson's easy access to so much land, he could keep shifters smuggling secretly with little threat of detection.

Daniel's return to Painter had shaken things up and cast a spotlight on Nelson. He'd evaded capture by purposefully diving over a waterfall last summer. It was a risky gamble, but they'd yet to find a body—man or mountain lion—so he was presumed alive and in hiding. Today, Heath and Daniel were continuing the searches they'd started months ago. They kept in touch with the local police and were going property by property to search for any signs of Nelson. They were headed to one of the few areas left that they hadn't searched before.

"Any more news from the police?" Heath asked.

He glanced over to see Daniel shrug. "Not really. I check in with Roger every few days. It's more of the same every time. They've searched almost every property now. They've found storage everywhere and even hauled in a few drug stashes. Seems like they were mostly running pills and heroin. Roger thinks one of the stashes closer to the Montana border came from that massive theft from the pharmaceutical company there. You remember hearing that on the news?"

"You mean those guys who cut a hole in the roof at one of those places and dropped in to pull out a couple million dollars worth of pills?"

"That's the one. Straight out of a movie. Anyway, Roger said they turned the stash over to the local authorities —the plan everywhere—and that's what they suspected. They'll report back after they sort it out. Can't believe the kind of money to be made from those."

Heath shook his head. He was sadly familiar with the kind of money to be made because he'd been so desperate for painkillers, he'd tried to score his own drugs. He still couldn't believe he'd fallen that far. A car accident and excruciating pain for months led him to a place he'd never imagined. Finally back on his feet, his mind clear and his body healthy, it was hard to imagine even now. In hindsight, he was relieved he'd gotten caught trying to score the pills because that's what put him back on track.

Daniel's voice nudged his thoughts back to the present. "Hey, I think we just passed the road."

Heath slowed his truck and eased onto the side of the highway to turn around. 'Really? I didn't see a damn thing."

"When I said it was an old logging road, I meant it was half-hidden in the trees and almost completely overgrown," Daniel said with a laugh.

Heath backed up and quickly angled the truck to turn around. In seconds, he saw the barely visible road Daniel mentioned. He turned into it, the tree braches giving way as the truck pushed through the opening. Once they were past the start of the road, it was less overgrown. The truck rocked as they rode along the bumpy gravel road. "How far in do you want to drive before we start scouting?"

"Maybe another mile or so. If Nelson's out here, he's not going to hang anywhere close to the highway."

"Of course. The police have already covered this area, right?"

Daniel nodded. "Yup, but it was over a month ago. They cleared out the storage, but they left the buildings intact. They've been trying to do that on the areas nearby because they figure Nelson's more likely to try to camp out close to Painter. Even though they've arrested most of the locals involved, he's still got a few friends who would help him around here."

"I'm sure he does." Heath glanced ahead to a clearing on the side of the road. It appeared to be a section of forest that had been logged within the last decade. Smaller trees were already filling the area, but there was room to park and turn around. "I'll park up ahead."

Moments later, they walked to the edge of the semi-cleared area and entered the thicker part of the forest. In silent agreement, they shifted. Heath let the power of the shift roll through him. His skin prickled as fur rippled over its surface. Once he was in full lion form, he lifted his nose and sniffed. Scents could be distinguished from great distances for mountain lions, as compared to humans. He was searching for the mingled scent of human and mountain lion. At the moment, all he got was the earthy scent of the forest and a cluster of deer somewhere in the vicinity. The deer would scatter once they sensed the presence of two shifters. Lion shifters rarely hunted the way wild mountain lions did because they had no need. Able to shift between human and lion form, they tended to only hunt in the wild if their survival depended on it, which was rare.

Daniel stretched beside him before he bolted off at a run. Heath had come to enjoy scouting with Daniel. For one, whenever Heath was in lion form, he felt stronger and stronger. It brought him back to the man and shifter he once was before his almost crippling car accident—powerful, dominant and proud. For another, it fed his cat's instinct to investigate and hunt. He didn't need to eat to satisfy that instinct. Lastly, getting to know Daniel's shifter side cemented Heath's confidence in him as his sister's mate. Heath didn't consider himself overbearing as an older brother, but he'd tear apart any man who hurt her. With Daniel, he knew he had nothing to worry about.

When they'd started scouting together after Nelson

disappeared, they agreed to stay together at all times. While they were both strong, dominant mountain lions, they weren't stupid and knew Nelson wouldn't hesitate to fight dirty. Nelson had almost sent Daniel and Sophia tumbling over that waterfall behind him, and Heath didn't doubt for a second it had been on purpose. For now, Heath and Daniel roamed through the forest, climbing higher and higher into the mountains surrounding Painter. Painter's location in the Rocky Mountains afforded a nearly ideal territory for mountain lion shifters, the ghost cats of the forest. The mountains were immense and created only pockets of land suitable for human dwelling. As such, there were massive tracts of rocky forest scattered along the mountain flanks. Shifters could live nearby and roam for days safely if they so chose.

For now, Heath and Daniel wove through the forest. They eventually came across an old cabin. The faded scent of human and lion lingered in the area. The cabin was empty, however faint tracks were visible in the dusty floor. They circled the nearby area. Heath froze when he sensed motion in the distance. Daniel came to his side and they backed into the shelter of a cluster of fir trees. In silence, they waited.

After several long moments, they saw a mountain lion padding quietly through the trees. Even though their view was limited, Heath didn't think it was Nelson. However, he knew by size and scent it was a male. The lion moved slowly and purposefully. Heath caught Daniel's eyes and shook his head. Daniel's return nod was imperceptible, but he confirmed Heath's opinion—this lion wasn't Nelson. For now, they simply watched. When the lion made it past them in the distance, they waited a few more moments before moving to follow him. The light was fading as the day turned to dusk. The trees cast long shadows in the forest with the lingering light from the sun falling in slants through the trees. The lion made his way toward the cabin. When he approached the small clearing, he paused and lifted his nose. In a flash, his head swung around and he bolted. Heath and Daniel leapt in unison, racing after him. He had just enough distance from them to disappear from view almost immediately.

The cool air ruffled through Heath's fur as he raced alongside Daniel. They threaded in and out of the trees. The lion cut a winding route through the forest, which they followed on scent alone until they reached the river—the same river Nelson had followed over the waterfall from miles away in the mountains. The lion's scent was lost once they crossed the river. Without a sound, they turned and made their way back.

Once they were back in Heath's truck and headed toward the farmhouse, Heath glanced over at Daniel. "That blows. Whoever that was, now he saw us, he'll probably move on."

Daniel shrugged. "I'm not too worried. Whoever we saw will show up again somewhere nearby. My bet is that shifter we just saw is helping Nelson. No reason to run unless he's got something to hide. Nothing I know about my uncle tells me he'll do anything the hard way. The hard way would be for Nelson to try to surface somewhere far away and start over. Nelson's lazy. He'd rather risk staying a little close and calling on the few friends he has left to get supplies to him."

Heath bit back the growl that rumbled in his throat and shook his head sharply. "Dammit! It would've been nice to at least catch up to that shifter and see if we could get any leads." He circled his hand on the steering wheel as he rounded a curve. Cresting a hill, the view opened up. Painter lay nestled in a valley. A mountain ridge rose behind the town. The sun was sliding behind the mountains, sending rays of gold mingled with orange and red into the sky above the mountains.

"Yeah, it would've been nice, but not likely. Nelson didn't stay hidden this long without being savvy, and the same goes for anyone helping him. I'm surprised that shifter didn't scent us sooner. If it weren't for the breeze blowing away from him, he probably would have."

"Right, right." Heath sighed as he turned onto Main Street. "Guess I was hoping for too much."

"Wasn't like I wasn't hoping either, but I'm relentlessly realistic. Or maybe pessimistic," Daniel offered wryly. "Don't forget to drop me off at the farmhouse."

Heath slowed abruptly as he was just about to pass the side road that led to the farmhouse. After dropping Daniel off, he headed toward downtown Painter. He was irritable about seeing that shifter and losing him like that, but he knew Daniel was right. Even once they narrowed down where Nelson was, he wasn't going to make it easy on them and nor would anyone helping Nelson. Heath made his way to Quinn's. He wasn't up for dinner alone tonight in his apartment. He parked across the street from Quinn's and headed inside. As usual, the place was bustling. A waitress racing by him caught his eye and nodded toward the bar. "Unless you want to wait a while, you might want to grab a seat at the bar."

There was a cluster of customers waiting to be seated in the front area. Heath threaded through them on his way toward the bar. He slid onto a barstool in the corner by the wall. He was content to eat in peace tonight. He snagged the menu tucked in between the condiments on the bar and perused it. At his name, he glanced up—straight into Vivi's bright blue eyes.

Chapter 6

Vivi stood across the bar from Heath, trying and failing to keep her body under control. His green gaze locked onto her, sending a rush of heat tumbling through her. She grabbed a towel and pointlessly wiped down the bar in front of him. "Here for dinner or just a drink?" she asked.

"Both," he replied, his voice gruff.

"You want the house draft?" Since she couldn't ignore small details about him, she remembered that was his usual order.

"Sure. That and a Quinn's burger."

She turned to the register by the wall and started to enter his order, only to have to re-enter it when she fumbled while she was typing. Her eyes collided with his again when she turned around, sending the heat simmering inside of her into a flash of flames. "Should be just a few minutes. I'll get your beer." She scurried away and quickly pulled a beer for him, only to forget to turn the tap off and spill beer on her hand. She swore to herself and grabbed a towel to wipe off her hand and his beer glass. *Get it together. Heath shows up and you turn into a bumbling fool.* She gave herself a mental shake and turned to hand his beer to him. When she was sliding it across the counter to him, another customer called her name, so she swung away immediately. The next little while passed in a blur. The customers just kept rolling in, which kept her busy. She didn't particularly like that she needed the extra cash from a few shifts a week at Quinn's, but she appreciated how the tips piled up and that she stayed so busy, she rarely thought about the time.

Tonight however, Heath's presence in the corner of the bar kept her skin prickling with awareness and her body suffused with heat. By the time her shift was about to end, she was in an all out war between her mind and body. Rationally, she just didn't know if letting much more happen with Heath was a good idea. He wasn't the kind of guy she could date and walk away from. He represented too much—she felt too much for him. He was her once upon a time high school crush from afar and a man she couldn't keep compartmentalized if things went sideways between them. That was her mind. As to her body...well, her body had all kinds of other ideas, most of them involving getting her hands on his sculpted body and diving into the desire shimmering around them.

She stepped into the back room behind the bar and snagged her jacket and purse. Dan, the bar manager, was busy stocking shelves with wine. He glanced up. "You outta here?"

"Yup. You need me to cover any nights next week?"

"If you want to cover the early shifts on Wednesday and Friday, they're yours."

"I'll take both nights." She started to turn and head out front, but she paused by the door and looked back to Dan. "Thanks for being so flexible with the schedule for me."

The clink of bottles continued as Dan set one bottle after another on the shelves. He shrugged and looked over his shoulder at her. "My mom raised me by herself, just like you're doing with Julianna. I get it. Whenever I have shifts open that work for you, they're yours. Plus, you work your tail off. No need to thank me."

"I get to thank you if I want, so deal with it."

"See you next week," he said with a wave and a chuckle.

Vivi pushed through the door back into the bustling bar. Her eyes automatically swung to the corner where Heath had been sitting. He wasn't there. Her heart sank. With her emotions a tornado inside, it was probably best he'd left. And yet…she'd been so damn hopeful she might have a few minutes alone with him tonight. She swallowed her sigh and tossed her fleece jacket over her shoulders as she threaded her way through the tables and customers to reach the door. She pushed through, the cool autumn air a contrast to the heat from inside the bar. She took a few steps beyond the door and paused on the sidewalk. The noise of the bar was muted now. She closed her eyes and took a deep breath, savoring the hint of wood smoke drifting from a nearby home.

"Hey there." Heath's voice was unmistakable, low and clear in the crisp night air.

Vivi opened her eyes and swung her head sideways to find Heath leaning against the building. His hands were tucked in the pockets of his jeans, tugging them low on his hips. Her heart gave a swift kick, jumpstarting her pulse. Heath pushed away from the wall, at which point she realized she'd yet to reply to him.

"Hey." One word was all she managed.

"I thought maybe I could give you a ride home."

The hope she'd knocked aside a few moments

earlier came roaring back. As usual, she'd walked into work after she'd dropped Julianna off at her mother's for the night. A ride home with Heath would mean she'd get far more than a few minutes with him. Her body took over, shoving her doubts out of mind. She nodded before she even realized it. Heath took another step closer to her. The streetlights glinted off his dark curls. His presence was potent, and she could feel the heat emanating off of him. He stood a mere foot or so away from her. The air felt electrified. She thought maybe she should move, but she couldn't.

He took another step closer. Her breath hitched and her belly clenched. "Is that a yes?" he asked, the rough edge of his voice sending prickles along her skin.

"Yes." Her voice was barely above a whisper.

For a long, sizzling moment, she thought he was going to kiss her. Her body nearly vibrated with tension. He didn't. Instead, he reached for her hand, curling his around it. Her breath came out in a slow sigh at the feel of his warm, strong grip. Without a word, he turned and walked toward his truck. She strode alongside him, her pulse pounding and need thrumming through her. Moments later, he eased his truck away from the curb. The short drive down Main Street to her home was quiet, the small space in his truck taut and the air fairly snapping with the currents between them.

Vivi glanced to Heath. His profile was silhouetted in the shadowed light, the angles of his face strong and clean. His nose had the barest jog along its bridge. She recalled he'd broken his nose when he fell off his bike in high school. His eyes canted to her, catching hers for a moment before he looked back at the road. In that tiny moment, liquid need swirled within her. Within minutes, they were at her house. Restless and jittery, she fumbled with the door handle. She felt Heath's palm curl around her arm.

"Hey," he said softly. "You okay?"

She let go of the handle and shifted in her seat, angling toward him. "Yeah. I, uh, I... Ugh. I'm a mess. I don't know what we're doing. I don't know what you want. I don't know..."

"Vivi." Heath said, his voice gravelly.

She whipped her gaze up, colliding with his. Her heart clenched. She bit her lip and tried to take a deep breath. Her pulse was racing, and she couldn't seem to get her body under control. Currents of need tossed wildly inside of her. Heath's hand eased its grip on her arm and slid up. She could feel the heat of his palm through her jacket.

Heath moved swiftly. Before she quite realized what was happening, he was opening the passenger door and helping her out. The door clicked shut behind her. Heath was right there in front of her. His eyes flashed in the light cast from her porch before his lips crashed against hers. In seconds, she was nearly on fire. His tongue tangled with hers in bold strokes. Their kiss went on and on. By the time he broke away, she was out of breath and surprised to discover she hadn't actually melted into a puddle.

He took a step back, the chilly air filling the space between them barely cooled the heat coursing through her. She grabbed his hand and tugged him along behind her. She almost stumbled racing up the steps. His palm curled around her hip, steadying her. "Easy."

Somehow they made it into the kitchen, while Jax raced past them out into the yard. By that point, Vivi had abandoned any restraint. She kicked her shoes off and tossed her jacket and purse on the counter. Heath was in the middle of tugging his jacket off when she stepped in front of him. She slid a palm up his chest and curled it around the back of his neck.

"Now."

He met her halfway, fitting his mouth over hers. The kiss that had begun outside continued. He swept his tongue inside her mouth, nipped at her lips and traced them. His hands roamed over her body, as hers did his. She savored the feel of the hard planes of his body under her touch, while the feel of his hands stroking down her back, cupping her bottom and curling around a breast was so delicious, she felt delirious.

She shoved his jacket off his shoulders, letting it fall to the floor. With a sigh, she slid her hands under his shirt and gasped at the warmth of his skin. He tore his lips away and blazed a wet trail down her neck. He broke free and held still, his eyes dark with need. The moment was hot and electric. Everything sped up. Clothes were torn off and tossed aside. The only light came from a lamp in the corner. Vivi snapped out of the haze of desire long enough to take in the sight of Heath. He wore nothing save a pair of black briefs. He was honed and sculpted. His years in the military were evident in the pure, raw muscle of his body. A ragged scar ran at an angle across his thigh, along with several precise, surgical scars—the permanent reminders of his brush with death. Her heart tightened when she recalled how close he'd come to not making it through to the other side of that car accident.

He stepped to her side, his hands tracing the curve of her waist. She stood almost bare before him, in white cotton underwear with red polka dots and a matching bra, both selected by Julianna once when they went shopping. She wanted everyone to wear polka dots, so Vivi obliged, figuring her underwear would never be seen. Now, she felt a twinge of embarrassment when Heath's eyes met hers with a gleam.

"I like your polka dots."

She flushed straight through and bit back a laugh. Heath traced her lips with his thumb before trailing it down along her neck and onto her shoulder. In slow motion, he hooked it under her bra strap and peeled it off her shoulder, the other following quickly. Her breasts tumbled loose, and she gasped in relief. Her nipples were so tight, they verged on pain. Heath's fingers traced lightly along the undersides of her breasts before circling her nipples. Her breath broke on a moan when his lips closed over one taut nipple. He swirled his tongue around it while teasing the other with his fingers. She lost herself in a haze of sensation, arching and flexing in his arms.

***

Heath dragged his eyes open. Vivi's hips were resting against the kitchen table. Her dark hair fell in a rumple around her shoulders. Her body was all lush curves and softness tempered with strength. She was bare except for her white and red polka dot panties, which somehow hit him right in the heart. She dragged a hand down his chest and stroked boldly over his briefs. What little control he had was almost lost when she curled her palm around his cock. He'd been throbbing with need for her for hours at this point, so it didn't take much to push him to the edge of his control.

He started to step back when she hooked her thumb over the waistband of his briefs and yanked them down. Before he could take a breath, she leaned forward and dragged her tongue along his cock. She teased him to near madness for several heated minutes while she explored him with her lips and tongue. A ragged groan broke free when she took him in her mouth. Hot, wet strokes of her tongue, the warm suction of her mouth and the grip of her palm, and he almost lost control. He yanked on the reins of his restraint and hung on—just barely.

He pulled her up and lifted her onto the table, while he simultaneously dragged her panties off with one hand and fumbled in the pocket of his jeans that were hanging over a chair by the table. His wallet fell to the floor when he tugged the condom out. He bumped heads with Vivi when she tried to helpfully roll the condom on. She giggled and glanced up, her blue eyes dark with passion and hinted with mirth. For a second, he froze. He was tossed asunder in the grip of pure lust mingled with an intimacy he'd never known with anyone.

Vivi's smile faded and her hand stilled. He nudged her chin up and caught her lips in another kiss. He stepped between her knees. She shimmied closer to the edge of the table when he reached between her legs and dragged his fingers through her folds. She was so wet, so ready. He stepped a fraction closer and nudged into her entrance.

"Vivi," he whispered.

He needed to see her. Her eyes opened, dark with a wild edge. Only then did he sheathe himself in her. She was tight and gasped when he seated himself fully within her. He held still, almost overcome at what it felt like to be this close to her. After several beats, he began to move. She curled her legs around his hips, her body flush against his. He held her hips as he surged again and again. He was so close to the edge, he could barely hold back. He slid a hand between them and circled it over her clit. Her eyes finally closed when her head fell back with her cry. Her channel clenched and throbbed around him. He finally let go, his release thundering through him. He dropped his head into the curve of her shoulder, his body shuddering from the echoes of his release.

Chapter 7

Vivi came awake slowly. She was curled on her side with Heath spooned behind her, his feet tangled with hers and his hand resting on her hip. The wispy light of dawn filtered through the curtains in her bedroom. Jax must have been sleeping on the other side of Heath because even though she couldn't see him, she could hear his purr rumbling through the room. She lay still, soaking in the feel of being skin to skin with Heath. She couldn't quite wrap her brain around what happened last night. Heath had blown past her barriers and made her youthful fantasies look weak. Just thinking about what it felt like to be with him flushed her. Restless, she shifted her legs.

"Mmm," Heath mumbled against her neck.

A shiver chased over her skin. His hand stroked up her side from her hip, following the dip of her waist, up along the side of her breast and over her shoulder. He brushed her tangled hair away from her face. Her belly fluttered and warmth spread through her. *Oh. Dear. God.* It felt so good to wake up with him like this.

He stretched behind her, his body going taut and

then relaxing against her again. "Mornin'," he said, his voice rough with sleep.

She rolled in his arms. His eyes were bright in the thin light. His dark curls were a wild mess. She couldn't help but smile at the sight of Heath sleepy. His mouth hooked at one corner. "What's so funny?"

She lifted a hand and ran it through his hair. "You have some serious bed head."

He chuckled. "Usually do. I wasn't much of a fan of the military buzz cut, but it did prevent this mess," he said, gesturing to his head.

Quiet fell between them. Jax's purr kept going. Heath glanced over his shoulder. "Wow, I'm surprised I didn't wake up."

She giggled. "Jax takes his purring very seriously. I've gotten so used to it, I hardly notice. When Julianna's home, he sleeps with her though."

"When do you need to pick her up?" he asked, his hand sifting through her hair.

"Oh, she takes the bus from my mom's straight to school. Since I usually work one shift during the school week, we have it all sorted out."

Heath nodded slowly. "Does that mean I can take you out to breakfast?"

She held his gaze, her heart clamoring for her to say yes, while her mind spun with worry. What if this didn't work out? What if she had to find a way to let her feelings go? It had all seemed so much easier when she'd kind of had a thing for him, but nothing had actually happened. Now, a lot more than something had happened. She didn't know how she could keep her feelings in a tidy corner anymore. She bit her lip and tried to take a breath to quell the anxiety rising up within her.

"Is breakfast okay?" he asked finally. When she

didn't reply right away, his hand stilled and he leaned up on his elbow. "Okay, spill it. What the hell are you thinking? I'm not a mind reader, but I can tell you're worried."

"I, um, I don't know. I'm not sure what we're doing and I don't know if it's a good idea…" She stumbled over her words and gulped in air. She had no idea how to contain her feelings for him and every little thing they shared only tightened the grip he had on her heart.

He held up a hand, and she quieted, somewhat relieved because she didn't know what the hell she meant to say.

"We blew way past breakfast last night. Maybe you're not sure what we're doing, but I am."

He sat up a little further, the sheet sliding down to his waist. He just had to go and do that. One look at him and her mouth went dry and longing coiled within her. His muscled chest and abs flexed as he slid up until he was leaning against the headboard. She pushed up on her elbow and sat up beside him, tucking the sheet up over her breasts.

When he spoke again, his voice was low and clear. "Back when I first kissed you, I meant what I said. I waited too damn long. I'm not after a fling. I'm after a lot more than that. I just didn't want to push too far or too fast."

Vivi thought her heart might pound its way out of her chest. Hope spun in circles inside, but she batted it back. She might have had a silly crush on Heath once upon a time, he might call to her like no other, but she wasn't a silly girl anymore. She didn't quite trust herself to know when she'd find the right mate for her. Because she'd been so wrong about Chris. She'd truly thought she'd found her mate in him—that shifter fantasy of another shifter who called to her like no other. In hindsight, what had blinded her were her own hopes and dreams and the need to prove to herself she could find another shifter who attracted her the way Heath did. Even though she'd tried to convince herself Chris did, it had never been the same.

To have Heath sitting here beside her now telling her he wanted a lot more than a fling, well, it flat out terrified her. Because what if she was wrong about him too? Oh, she trusted him to be good to her and not blow in and out of her life. She knew him to be a man and shifter of honor, but what if she didn't turn out to be what he hoped for? What if this was just a passing blip of pure lust?

"Vivi?"

Heath's voice nudged her out of her thoughts. She glanced over at him. His eyes never broke away. She couldn't quite find her words.

He reached over and curled his hand around hers. The warmth and strength of his grip anchored her and soothed the unsettled feeling inside. "I'm not going to take off on you like Chris did. You have to know that," he said, his words firm.

Her throat was tight. She swallowed against the feeling and took in a gulp of air. "I know you wouldn't do that, but what if this doesn't work out? I can't really avoid you if things go wrong—it'll be weird. It's not simple being a single mother either. I have to think about Julianna. I don't want to confuse her, or..." She paused and forced herself to take another breath. She didn't quite know how to tell him she just couldn't take it if it turned out he didn't want to stay with her. She didn't do casual, she never had.

"I know we have to think about Julianna. Even if I know precisely what I want, I have enough sense to know we have to take it one step at a time. Can you just try to trust me that I know what we have here?"

Tears pressed at the back of her eyes, but she held the feeling inside. She wasn't going to fall apart right now.

It would be far too mortifying for Heath to see just how vulnerable she felt with him. She glanced over. "Is this one of those things where you think you found your mate?" Her question was tinged with sarcasm.

Heath didn't flinch. He nodded firmly. "Don't make light of it. You didn't with Sophia, so don't do it with yourself. It's not like we barely know each other. If last year hadn't been such a mess for me, I'd have let you know how I felt a hell of a lot sooner. I had to know I could be the man you deserved before I did that. Can we just enjoy that we had an amazing night and have some breakfast? I thought you needed to know how I felt, so you didn't start wondering what I wanted. I can wait until you're ready though."

His words hit her right in her center. He was so clear, so definite. While she was a muddle inside. Even though she knew she wanted him, she also knew it wouldn't help to ruminate on her worries just now. She'd practice taking it one step at a time. She met his eyes and nodded. "How about we have breakfast here? I'll cook." At his grin, she kicked the covers free.

***

Heath pushed through the door at the bank and walked briskly to his truck. He tossed the folder of papers on the seat and closed the door. He paused on the sidewalk and glanced around. Painter was nestled in a valley with mountains surrounding it. Main Street was picturesque with quaint, colorful storefronts. A gust of wind sent leaves spinning in a swirl. He stepped off the sidewalk and looked both ways before striding across the street to Mile High Grounds. The bell jangled above the door when he entered. It was late afternoon and the coffee shop was quieter than at most hours. A few college students were nursing coffees while they studied and there was a knitting group in the corner. His sister glanced up from the counter.

"Hey Heath! How's it going?"

He reached the counter. "It's going pretty damn good. Just got the bank loan approved to get my construction business started. I thought the paperwork would never end, but it's official as of a few minutes ago."

Sophia squealed and clapped her hands. "Yippee! I know you wanted to get that taken care of. So what does it mean?"

"It means I've got seed money to invest in the heavier equipment I need. I've already been picking up jobs, but I had to keep it small. Now, I can take on bigger jobs and hire a team when I've got enough work to make it worthwhile."

Sophia grinned and leaned a hip against the counter. "You can use my accountant if you want."

Heath chuckled and kicked his toe against the floor. "I'll probably take you up on that."

"It's Sara Willis. Her office is just a few doors down the street. She's awesome and so picky it's annoying. I figure picky's good when it comes to accounting. Anyway, coffee?"

"Of course. Just something dark today. Nothing sweet."

"Got it!" Tommy called out from behind the espresso machine.

Heath glanced around the room, half hoping to see Vivi walk through the door. He'd barely been able to keep her out of his mind since last night and this morning. A few hours of hard work on a small decking job kept him from spinning circles inside. He'd been distracted at the bank meeting, but fortunately all the details had already been hammered out.

"Looking for Vivi?"

He whipped his head back to Sophia to find her grinning.

"No, I…" He paused with a shake of his head. "Actually, yes. I thought she might be by this afternoon."

"Logical guess, seeing as she stops by here most afternoons."

Tommy stepped to the counter and slid Heath's coffee across. He glanced between them. "Yeah, we both noticed you can hardly keep your eyes off Vivi lately."

Heath almost choked on his sip of coffee. Sophia started to laugh and immediately covered her mouth when he glared at her. Tommy turned away and headed to the back room, but not before tossing a sly grin over his shoulder. "Gotta play those cards closer to your chest if you don't want anyone to notice."

When Tommy disappeared through the door into the back, Sophia's expression sobered. "So, you and Vivi?"

Heath wasn't ready to tell his little sister about last night, but he wasn't going to hide his feelings. He nodded and took a gulp of his coffee, savoring the rich flavor.

Sophia looked at him for a long moment, her eyes searching and considering. "She means a lot to you."

"She does." His heart tightened. Last night had taken the hints of his feelings and ratcheted up their intensity.

Sophia watched him for another moment. Her breath came out on a sigh. "Oh. Does she know how you feel?"

He shrugged. "Maybe. I tried to let her know, but I'm not so sure how much she's ready to hear."

Sophia was quiet for several beats. "Give her time."

"That's it? Give her time?"

Sophia gave him a small smile and shrugged.

"That's it. It may not sound like much, but she's been on her own for years. After the way things went with Chris, she's wary. If you don't give her time, she'll get in her own way."

At that moment, another customer approached the counter and Heath stepped out of the way. "I'll probably be by again soon," he said with a lift of his coffee cup.

"I'll be here. Maybe you can meet Daniel and I for dinner tomorrow."

"Just tell me where."

At that, he turned and left. As he was walking back across the street, Daniel's truck passed by. He came to a quick stop and waved to Heath as he rolled down his window.

"What's up?" Heath said when he reached Daniel's truck.

"I was just about to call you. Roger wants us to stop by. They've caught a few leads north of town."

"You got it. I'll meet you there."

A short while later, Heath leaned against the wall in Roger Shaw's office. Roger was the lead investigator on the various cases associated with the smuggling network. He and a few other officers were shifters, which came in quite handy during the months of searching for Nelson.

"To keep it short, we've been revisiting the properties around town, and we're pretty sure someone's living in the old buildings on the main property where your grandfather's offices were. It's one of the first places we checked out. I figured all along Nelson and anyone helping him would wait it out and loop back this way."

"What now?" Daniel asked.

"Since you guys have been searching, I thought it'd be best if we made sure we're covering different areas. I'd prefer if we planned a rotation. I also followed up on that shifter you saw last week. My best guess is it's Chris Barnett. He's…"

"Vivi's ex," Heath interjected. "Why do you think it's him?" Heath had never even met Chris. Vivi had dated Chris and had Julianna while Heath was away in the military. He'd come home on leave during that time, but he'd never actually met Chris.

"One of the guys we're holding on charges for dealing thinks it's him. The guy said Chris handled some of the pick ups in this area. After he moved away from Painter, he got picked up for dealing in Boulder. He bounced back here and a buddy of mine on the force there gave us a heads up to keep an eye on him when things heated up with the smuggling network," Roger explained.

Heath shifted his shoulders against the wall, considering what it might mean to Vivi to learn Julianna's father was involved in the smuggling network. "Are you gonna try to bring him in?" Heath asked.

Roger nodded. "Of course. I was actually hoping you guys could help with that. Since he didn't seem to know who you were, he got flushed out. He definitely knows who we are. I was thinking you guys could keep scouting over on that side of town and we'll focus on the other side and north."

Daniel was nodding along and asking questions, while Heath considered how to talk to Vivi about this. He didn't want her to find out some other way, but he worried about how she'd react. He'd gathered enough threads of information to understand things didn't go well between her and Chris. Chris's complete absence from Julianna's life had led Heath to conclude Chris wasn't worth much, but he could only guess how Vivi felt about that. It infuriated him Chris had been so careless toward Vivi and Julianna.

"Heath?"

Daniel's voice cut into his thoughts. "Sorry. What?"

"I was just telling Roger we'd plan to scout in that area once every few days. That works for you, right?"

"Oh yeah. No problem."

A few minutes later, Heath walked at Daniel's side out to the parking lot. "So, uh, I'm thinking I need to give Vivi a heads up about Chris."

Daniel leaned against his truck. "I'd say so. If she hears about it from someone else, she'll be pissed we didn't tell her. There's that and the fact he might show up around town."

Heath nodded. "Right."

Daniel arched a brow. "I'm leaving this one up to you. I could let Sophia know and she'd tell Vivi, but then…"

Heath finished his sentence for him. "Vivi will wonder why the hell I didn't say something."

Chapter 8

A remote powered toy car zoomed past Vivi's foot, buzzing as it rolled around the room. Vivi's mother, Evelyn Sheldon, stood by the sink in her kitchen and glanced over at Vivi.

"She can't get enough of that car. It makes babysitting easy. All we do is hand her the remote and she's off," Evelyn said with a smile. She shook the water from her hands and snagged a towel to dry them.

"I know. I promised her we'd get one for home." Vivi glanced through the archway into the living room where Julianna stood by the windows, grinning as she guided the remote car around the legs of the coffee table. Vivi turned back at the sound of her mother's footsteps. Her mother stepped over to the kitchen table. Evelyn was tall and elegant and moved with fluid grace. Vivi had inherited her mother's almost black hair and blue eyes, but she wasn't quite as tall. Evelyn sat down across from her. Vivi had stopped by to pick Julianna up after school. She'd gotten tied up longer than usual at a landscaping job, so she'd called the school and asked them to make sure

Julianna was dropped off at her parents' house.

Her mother leaned back in her chair. "So, how is Heath doing these days?"

It wasn't unusual for her mother to ask about Heath. With Vivi and Sophia practically joined at the hip growing up, their families had become close. Yet, her mother had no clue Vivi had spent a mind-blowing, body-melting, heart-spinning night with Heath. If her mother had ever picked up on Vivi's youthful crush on Heath years ago, she'd never let on. Just hearing Heath's name sent a hot rush through Vivi, her body immediately recalling the feel of him against her and within her. Vivi mentally shook herself. She couldn't get all moony and ridiculous over Heath simply because her mother asked how he was doing.

She fiddled with her bracelet. "He seems to be doing great. He's helping Daniel a lot out at his grandparents' old farmhouse. Daniel wants to have it ready for him and Sophia to move in by winter."

"That's a lovely old place. I'm glad to hear Heath's staying strong. It's been a rough year since his car accident."

Vivi switched from fiddling with her bracelet to picking up an apple from the bowl of fruit on the table and rolling it back and forth between her hands. "Yeah, I'd say he's completely back on his feet."

Vivi felt her mother's assessing eyes on her. "You know, it's nice to see Sophia find someone. I don't suppose finding someone is on your radar?"

Vivi focused on the apple rolling back and forth in her palms. "What do you mean?" she finally asked, although she knew perfectly well what her mother was asking. For a while after she had Julianna, her mother stayed quiet about any possibility of a relationship for Vivi. But the past year or so, she'd bring it up occasionally and ask why Vivi didn't even date anyone. Vivi's parents had married young and loved each other deeply. Her father was away a lot for work as a commercial airline pilot, yet his absences seemed to only tighten the bonds between them. Vivi wasn't quite up for a discussion about her mother's hopes and dreams for Vivi to find her own meant-to-be love.

Evelyn tilted her head to the side. "You're purposefully being obtuse. You know what I mean. It'd be nice for you to give...well, anyone a chance. I know we've already talked about it, but it's silly for you to keep the whole world out. You deserve the chance to find a good man and it wouldn't hurt Julianna to have a father around."

A flash of anger rose inside Vivi, anger with herself for falling for Chris. She hadn't seen past the surface. Julianna was only now getting old enough to ask questions about her father. Vivi didn't want her to harbor negative feelings, but she kept stumbling over how to explain his absence to Julianna without hurting her. She met her mother's eyes and sighed. "Look Mom, maybe I am, but it's not that simple. Even if your whole fantasy fluff idea about love with the right mate works out for me, Julianna technically has a father. Sure, it'd be great for her to have someone actually filling that role, but it makes things complicated."

"Life is complicated all by itself. I know Julianna technically has a father, but he's never behaved like a father. Chris is basically a sperm donor. His absence shouldn't keep you from finding someone for yourself. I know you don't like to talk about it, but tell me why you don't even want to try."

Vivi set the apple in the bowl again and switched to sliding her bracelet in a slow circle around her wrist. The cool silver was smooth against her skin. She sighed. "It's not that I don't even want to try, it's just thinking about it stresses me out."

Evelyn's blue eyes were warm and concerned. She was quiet for a moment. "Maybe you should stop thinking so hard."

"That's what landed me with Chris. I wasn't thinking."

Evelyn rolled her eyes. "I meant stop thinking about how hard it might be to bring someone into your life. Just relax and see what happens. At least be open to possibilities. I'm sure you gave the same advice to Sophia last year. She was so tied up in worrying about her brother, she barely let life happen."

Vivi couldn't help but laugh. "So I did, so I did. Fine then. I'll try to relax and see what happens." Another memory of the other night rose in her mind. She'd definitely relaxed. A small part of her wanted to talk to her mother about Heath, but she wasn't quite ready to go there. If her mother had an inkling of what was going on with Vivi and Heath, she'd never let it go. If things didn't work out with them, it would be more than awkward. *Right. See this is exactly why you need to be careful.*

Vivi gave another mental shake to knock her mind off its loop. At that moment, the remote car came zipping into the kitchen again and bounced against the refrigerator. Julianna was right behind it. She stopped by Vivi's chair and leaned on her knee. Vivi stroked Julianna's dark hair. "Hey sweetie. Just a few more minutes, okay?"

Julianna glanced up and nodded. "I know. You said only 'til five. It says five," she said, gesturing to the clock on the wall above the stove.

Vivi glanced at the clock and smiled slowly. "So I did. How about you put up your car for Gram before we go?"

"Okay." Julianna remained where she was, her elbow hooked over Vivi's knee. Her slight weight was warm against Vivi's leg. She let her free arm swing back and forth, the remote controller held loosely in her hand. After a moment, she pushed away and ran over to pick up the toy car. She walked quickly to the pantry in the corner of the kitchen and carefully placed the car and its remote control in a box on the bottom shelf.

Evelyn glanced from Julianna to Vivi and smiled softly. "She is so much like you."

"You say that all the time."

Evelyn shrugged. "Because it's so true. Just like you, she's mostly well-behaved, but she's got that willful streak. I like that part best."

Vivi laughed softly. "Most of the time that streak isn't a problem. Unless she gets in a battle of wills like she did last year with her teacher."

Her mother shrugged again. "It passed. When it comes to girls, a tough side is a good thing."

Julianna walked back across the room, twisting one of her braids around her hand. Vivi watched her, her heart swelling the way it did only when it came to her daughter —her wild, willful, and mostly obedient little girl. "That it is," Vivi said, catching her mother's eyes as she stood up from the table.

***

Heath's boot slipped on the bottom rung of the ladder. He stumbled slightly as he caught his footing on the ground. Rain had begun to fall steadily within the last half hour. He'd been working on a garage job. He'd hoped to finish the framing for the roof today, but it was too wet to keep going safely. He quickly took down the ladder and loaded it on his truck. By the time he finished putting away the rest of the tools, he was soaked. Driving along Main Street, his eyes caught on a flash of bright red. When he turned to look, he realized it was Vivi. She was tugging the hood of her red raincoat over her head and jogging down the street. He immediately swung over and reached across to open his door. "Vivi!"

She slowed and glanced to the side, her eyes widening when she saw him. She came to a stop, huddling inside her raincoat. "Hey," she said, her words muted through the fall of rain pattering on his truck.

"How about a ride?" he asked, gesturing to the passenger seat.

She stood there long enough that he wasn't sure she'd accept his offer. Just when he was about to ask again, she stepped to the truck and climbed in. After she closed the door, she pushed her hood back. Her hair was damp and a drop of water rolled down her cheek. She lifted the edge of her shirt and swiped it over her face. "I'm soaked. Hope you don't mind if I get your seat wet."

He chuckled. "I'm probably wetter than you."

She glanced over, a slow smile spreading across her face. "Were you out working when the rain started?"

"Oh yeah. It was just a drizzle at first, so I kept going. Not the best idea because next thing I knew it was pouring."

Heath put his truck in gear and looked to the side before he pulled back onto the street. Vivi was quiet during the short drive to her house. When he pulled up in her driveway, she glanced over. His entire body tightened. With her dark hair curling in damp tendrils around her face, her blue eyes stood out in the gray light. Her jacket had fallen open. The damp fabric of her t-shirt outlined the curves of her breasts and her taut nipples. A bolt of lust shot through him. *Oh hell. All Vivi has to do is exist and you forget everything.* He batted back at the cynical voice in his head. He heard her take a breath and swung his eyes up.

"Do you want to come in?" she asked.

Her question was rather pointless. If she invited him anywhere, he'd go. Because all he wanted was to be with her. Over the year, he'd thought about her time and again, but he kept telling himself he had to wait. After he'd managed to pull the scattered pieces of his life together since the accident and finally felt like he was on his way back from the shadows, he'd had a glimmer of what might lie between them. But then he'd gone and kissed her— again and again. It set the floodgates loose and he'd known his heart belonged only to one woman. It was said to be that way for shifters sometimes, but even before his accident, Heath had a mildly cynical view of that. Now, with his desire and feelings unfurling within, he knew with certainty what Vivi was to him.

She looked away and started to pull her raincoat tighter. She reached for the door handle. "Well, uh, thanks for the ride…"

"Wait. I'm coming in. I guess I thought I said so."

Her eyes widened and a sigh escaped. "Oh. Okay. Let's get inside then."

They dashed through the rain, which had started to fall more heavily on the drive to her house. Once they were inside, Vivi hung her raincoat up and kicked off her shoes, gesturing for him to do the same. She walked between the living room and kitchen, flicking on a few lamps, before leaning against the kitchen counter and eyeing him. "How about I make us some dinner?"

"I'll never say no to food. When will Julianna be home?"

"Oh, she's having dinner and movie night with my mom. They do it once a month on Fridays."

"Sounds fun."

Vivi smiled. "They both love it." She pushed away from the counter and turned to open the refrigerator. "Let's see what we have."

She wore a pair of navy leggings with one of those fitted t-shirts she favored, this one bright purple. His eyes traced the lines of her legs up to the lush curve of her hips. Without thinking, he took a few strides to reach her and stroked his hands along her waist and over her hips. His heart thundered and want coiled inside. He heard her take a quick breath. She let the refrigerator door fall closed and turned in his arms. Her eyes slammed into his. He could see the flutter of her pulse in her neck. When she lifted a hand and stroked it up his chest, he let go and crashed his lips against hers. He cupped her bottom and tugged her close, groaning into her mouth at the feel of her soft and strong body flexing against him.

He dove into the warm sweetness of her mouth. She met him stroke for stroke. Desperate for more, he drew back and buried his face in her neck, inhaling the scent of her—a hint of lavender mingled with the cool rain lingering on her skin. He lifted her in his arms and headed straight for her bedroom, trailing hot kisses along her neck as he strode quickly to her room and shouldered through the door. His knees bumped the edge of the bed. He kept his hold on her and slowly eased her down. He stood and yanked his shirt off. She leaned up and followed suit, tossing her shirt to the floor and shimmying out of her leggings. She wore another polka dot bra—the dots bright green on this one. She'd explained the fateful shopping trip when Julianna had insisted everything they buy have polka dots. His heart clenched at the sweetness of that.

His eyes on her, he dropped a knee on the bed and placed his palm on her chest, slowly pushing her back on the bed. For a moment, he sensed hesitation. Then she relaxed and stretched out. He looked at her, her dark hair still damp from the rain spread out in a tangle on the bed, her body all soft curves tempered with strength. Female shifters were remarkably strong and Vivi was no exception. He curled a palm over her calf and slid up the soft skin, savoring her quick intake of breath. He kept moving, stroking over her thigh and letting his fingers trail across her panties. He could feel the wet heat through the cotton and had to fight to hold back from tearing them off and plunging inside of her. She shifted restlessly.

He hooked his thumb over the edge of her panties and dragged them off. With a kick, she sent them flying to the corner. He stroked into her cleft, slick with moisture. A low moan broke from her throat when he delved into her channel. She was so wet, he almost came in his jeans. He hung on, but just barely. He nudged her knee to the side and leaned forward to taste her.

***

Vivi almost came instantly. She'd been simmering with need since the moment she'd climbed into his truck. Heath's fingers stroked into her channel, and she arched into his touch. Between his tongue and fingers, he drove her wild. Her hips moved of their own accord, responsive to every subtle touch. She distantly heard her broken cries and Heath's name falling from her lips. Diving into sensation, she chased the pleasure. He brought her higher and higher, the need tightening within, until he dragged his tongue across her clit. She flew apart, spikes of pleasure coursing through her. His mouth stilled, and he slowly pulled away. She dragged her eyes open to see him stand and swiftly shove his jeans down. He swiped them up to yank a condom out of his pocket. His eyes lifted and locked onto hers, his gaze hot and electric. She couldn't have looked away if she tried.

The mattress dipped when his knee rested against it. He stretched over her, his hands capturing hers and his elbows bracketing her face. She curled into his grip when he laced his fingers with hers. Her pulse lunged and her belly tightened with need. She could feel his hard shaft against her. Her body was still shuddering from the echoes of her climax. She was so sensitive that the subtle shift of his hips sent another shock of pleasure through her. His eyes never left hers, and her heart felt cracked open. He dipped his head and brought his lips to hers—the briefest of kisses—and then pulled back. Her breath came in shallow pants and her body drew tight, the anticipation notching her need higher and higher. Reflexively, she arched into him and he surged inside, seating himself deeply. She gasped and her eyes fell closed.

He felt so good—so, so good. But it wasn't just the physical. It was the near burning incandescence between them—a mingling of pure physical need and emotional passion. He held still for a heated moment and then began to move—long, slow, deep surges. He rolled his hips against her as she rose to meet each thrust. Heat twisted inside of her. Tremors built from the lingering pulses of her climax. His eyes burned into her—dark and intent. Her core drew tight as he began to move faster and faster. She curled her legs around his hips, urging him on until he was drumming into her. Chasing the sweet, hot release, she arched into him when he dipped his head and captured her nipple. With a swirl of his tongue, he bit into her softly, right when he slammed his hips into hers again. Her release thundered through her. A raw cry tore from her throat. He lifted his head and tightened his hands in hers. One more deep stroke, and his body went rigid before he shuddered and fell against her with a muffled groan.

His hands eased in hers, and he slid to her side. They lay still, tangled and damp. Heath's heartbeat pounded against her side. Her breath slowed in unison with his. When she turned her head and found his green gaze, a rush of intimacy washed through her. She felt unmoored, wild and untethered inside. He was quiet and still, but then he moved suddenly. He gathered her in his arms and stood. Without a word, he walked to the bathroom adjacent to her bedroom. He flicked the light on and slowly eased her down. Within seconds, he'd turned the shower on and steam started to fill the room. He stepped inside, tugging her in behind him. With hot water cascading around them, he slid his hands through her hair and looked into her eyes. Caught in the intimacy of his gaze, a sense of panic started to rise. Almost as if he could read her mind, he stroked a hand down her spine, his touch soothing her.

Chapter 9

Heath leaned forward and set his empty plate on the coffee table. After they showered, Vivi had thrown together some sandwiches. They were in the living room on the couch. Jax had curled up in the corner and was busy grooming himself after coming in drenched from the rain. Vivi stood and picked up Heath's plate, carting it into the kitchen along with hers. She returned with a bottle of wine and two glasses. He watched while she filled them, her damp hair falling over her shoulders as she leaned forward. She'd changed into a pair of swingy cotton pants and a sweatshirt. He'd run out to his truck to grab the change of clothes he kept there. He'd been doing construction long enough to know it was smart to keep something clean on hand, so he was in a faded pair of jeans and a clean flannel shirt. Vivi had kindly tossed his wet clothes in the washer.

All in all, the entire evening was feeling so domestic, he felt unsettled. He might know precisely where he hoped to go with Vivi, but this felt almost too good to be true. His mind was also turning over how he was going to tell her about Roger's suspicions about Chris. He didn't want to wait too long and risk her hearing about it from someone else. When she plunked onto the couch and held out a glass of wine for him, he took it from her and immediately took a healthy swallow.

"I have some news from Roger," he said, electing to take the quick, direct approach.

She leaned into the cushions and crossed her legs. She looked so relaxed, he wanted to take back his words. Vivi relaxed wasn't something he got to enjoy often. She was usually humming with energy. Over the last few months, when she was around him, she also had a guarded edge to her. Right now, her hair fell in a rumpled tousle around her shoulders. Her eyes were warm and the lines of tension had disappeared from her face. Much as he was tempted to forget what he was about to say, she needed to hear it and he'd rather she hear it from him.

She snagged a soft knit blanket off the back of the couch and tucked it over her lap as she sipped her wine. "Any news would be good. It feels like we've heard nothing but more of the same for months."

"Right. Well, I'm not sure what you're gonna think of this. You know Daniel and I've been scouting the nearby areas?" At her nod, he continued. "A few days ago, we headed out to one of the properties the police searched months ago. We saw a shifter out there, a male I wasn't familiar with. It definitely wasn't Nelson, but whoever it was didn't want to be found. Anyway, we reported back to Roger, and..." He paused and ran a hand through his hair, his stomach knotting with tension. There was no easy way to tell her Julianna's father was suspected of being part of the shifter smuggling network and damn if he knew how to soften the blow. He took another gulp of his wine and continued. "Roger thinks it's likely it was Chris."

Vivi's eyes widened and her hand flew to her

mouth. "What?! Oh my God. Please tell me that can't be right. Why does Roger think it's him?" She took a healthy swallow of her wine, her eyes pinned to Heath.

"Because one of the guys they arrested recently said it was probably Chris. Apparently, Chris was doing pick ups for Nelson. I know you haven't been in touch with him…"

Vivi cut in. "Not in over three years. Once he found out I was pregnant, he pretty much bolted. I figured out he wasn't the greatest guy, but… Oh hell. Just tell me everything Roger knows."

"Aside from what they learned about him working locally for Nelson, apparently he was arrested for dealing in Boulder. When he made his way back to Painter, the police in Boulder gave the guys here a heads up because of everything going on with the smuggling network. That's all Roger knows."

Vivi leaned back into the cushions again and sighed. "This sucks. I've accepted Chris isn't interested in being a father, but it doesn't change the fact he's Julianna's father. She asks about him sometimes and I never know what to say. I can't tell her that her dad's a loser who can't be bothered. Now I have to worry about him being involved in the smuggling network. I mean, that's awful. Those shifters have put us all at risk. If we didn't have shifters on the police force here, we'd have a real problem. As it is, they're doing everything they can to keep it quiet that it's shifters. Now I know just what a scumbag Chris really is."

Heath didn't know what to say. He wanted to promise her it would be okay, but he couldn't. He could keep Vivi and Julianna safe from a lot of things, but not from the realities of Chris's risky and damning choices. Cold anger knotted inside. He detested the kind of man Chris was. It made him sick to consider how Chris had hurt

Vivi and essentially abandoned Julianna. He looked over at Vivi. Her eyes were bright with tears. He started to reach for her, but she shook her head sharply. Swiping at her eyes, she gulped in air.

"It's just one more thing to figure out how to explain to Julianna when she's old enough to understand. You have no idea how much I wish I could go back and have enough sense to see Chris for who he was. I say that and then I remember that not for a second would I change the events that brought Julianna into my life. I just wish I could have her, and she could also have a father who wasn't a complete asshole and who cared enough to be around."

Heath absorbed what she said and bit back his words. He wanted to tell her it would be okay because he'd be the father to Julianna she didn't have, but he figured that might be pushing too far and too fast for Vivi right now. At the moment, she needed time to come to terms with what Chris might be doing. "You know, it might be Chris or it might not. They won't really know until they bring him in."

Vivi shrugged. "My guess is it's him. I never mentioned it, but here and there, I wondered if he was involved in something like this. I didn't want to believe it, but he was always looking for the easy way and he didn't care much for any kind of responsibility. That's how he approached the whole father thing. He acted like it was a burden on him. When I told him I was pregnant, that was it. Maybe if I'd decided against having Julianna, it would have been different, but I doubt it. Smuggling would appeal to him because it was good money and risky. It doesn't surprise me to hear he got picked up for dealing in Boulder. I just want him arrested. I want it over, so I can know for sure. It's not like I'll tell Julianna about this now, but it'll give me a few years to figure out how the hell to tell her not only does her father not give a damn about her, but he's also a criminal."

Vivi's voice was bitter and weary. Heath's mind spun as he considered how he could make this right. Yet, there was no making it right. It was what it was. Whether or not Chris was involved in the smuggling network, it didn't change what Julianna would have to accept about her father overall. The knot of anger tightened further. Heath might not be able to make it right, but it didn't change how furious he was about it. He looked over at Vivi and stretched his arm across the back of the couch, his hand curling around the nape of her neck. This time she didn't push him away. She relaxed into his touch as he slowly massaged her neck, easing the tension bundled there.

After several quiet moments, Jax's purr started. Heath chuckled. "Jax is the Olympic champ of purring."

Vivi rolled her head to the side, a slow smile curling the corners of her mouth. "So he is." She paused and took a deep breath. "Thanks for telling me about Chris. I know you didn't have to."

"There was never any question. I figured you had to know soon."

She held his gaze for a long moment. His body started to tighten and that familiar need coursed through him.

***

The following afternoon, Vivi drove along the winding highway. The road hugged the mountainside. Leaves fluttered in the breeze. The road was dappled with the shadows of trees and blowing leaves. As she drove along, the tension in her stomach knotted tighter and tighter. She hadn't told anyone she was coming out here, but she was determined to find Chris herself. She didn't think he would hurt her, but she wanted to talk to him.

Heath had told her where he and Daniel had gone searching the other day, so she knew she was looking for an old overgrown road that led into the forest. In her years growing up in Painter, she and Sophia had explored almost every nook and cranny in the mountains surrounding Painter. She recalled this old logging property from back when Daniel's grandfather was actively working on the land. She'd hated seeing the barren sections of land, absent of trees. She'd been relieved when they'd stopped logging. It had been years since she'd explored over on this side of town, but she knew where to look. The overgrown road was right where she remembered. She turned into it slowly. Broken branches and foliage cued her it was the right road since Heath and Daniel had driven through here already.

She followed their tire tracks to where they must have parked in a small clearing. The clearing had once held a few temporary buildings where the heavy duty logging equipment was stored. She climbed out of her car and paused beside it. The autumn air was chilly, its scent crisp and refreshing. The forest rose tall around the edges of the clearing. She walked through the clearing and into the trees. Sunlight fell through the trees, slanting rays of light brightening the forest. She held still for a moment and then shifted. Power whipped through her. In seconds, she stretched in her cat form. The soft breeze ruffled through her fur. She stood tall and sniffed the air, hoping to catch any hint of Chris nearby. No luck. She scented nothing other than the earthy hint of autumn and leaves blowing on the breeze.

She glanced around and started running slowly through the forest. She recalled there were some caves in an area a few miles from here. She didn't know where Chris might be hiding out, but she figured she'd start where he could find shelter. She wove through the trees, picking up speed as she moved. A pair of squirrels chattered at her from a tree as she passed by them.

The terrain became rockier as she ascended deeper into the mountains. She moved quickly and quietly, her senses attuned to any changes around her. As she approached the area where the caves were, a gust of wind blew through the trees. She scented another shifter. Coming to an abrupt stop, she waited quietly. A crow called nearby. A chipmunk scampered across the ground in front of her, pausing to stare at her for a moment before dashing between two boulders. Her skin prickled as she sensed the other lion getting closer.

She held still for a moment before she leapt, almost silently, into a tree branch. The height afforded her a better view through the trees, and she spied the other cat padding quietly through the trees. At first, she didn't have a clear view, but as the shifter moved closer, she could see it was Chris. She hadn't harbored much hope, but what little she had, she'd been clinging to tightly. She'd hoped against hope that she was wrong about Chris and he hadn't been stupid enough to get involved in the smuggling network. She didn't want Julianna to have to learn that detail about her father later on. As she released that tiny bit of hope, fury rose on its heels. Without thinking, she coiled and leapt to the ground, dashing through the trees and heading straight for Chris.

She closed the distance between them swiftly, giving up any attempt at stealth. Chris swung around and growled when she wove through the trees and bolted onto the bluff where he was walking. She didn't hold back and snarled as she went for him, claws extended as she caught him in the shoulder. She knew he recognized her because he hesitated for a split second before snarling in return when he dodged her. She swiped at him again, this time catching him solidly in the neck. He growled and went for her in return. What had initially been a half-hearted fight on his part swung to fierce, his desperation showing. She was driven by her own fury, fury formed from the festering anger she'd held inside for years—anger at herself for falling for Chris and anger at him for not giving a damn about Julianna.

Vivi dodged and swirled as Chris fought with her. Even though they'd dated and she'd traveled in the mountains a few times with him in lion form, she'd never seen him fight. He was sloppy, but strong. She pushed and pushed until she almost had him cornered among a cluster of boulders. Just when she thought she could subdue him, he lunged and sunk his claws into her shoulder. Searing pain shot through her, and she cried out. He gained just enough leverage to pin her. Fear rose within, riding the fumes of her adrenaline. She didn't give up though and snarled, swiping her claws across his face.

Chris released her and stepped away. He gave her a long look before he bolted and raced through the trees. She scrambled to her feet and started to take chase before she stopped. She didn't know what she meant to do. She'd come out here because she needed to know if it was Chris. She had her answer. Only her festering anger was driving her to fight. She could keep chasing him, but she didn't think she'd manage to subdue him on her own and bring him in. Her breath misted in the chilly air. She heard Chris running, the sound of him weaving through the trees fading as he got further and further away. She turned and headed back to her car. Her shoulder was burning with pain from the deep gouge of his claws. The concrete, physical pain mirrored her emotional state—anger mingled with sadness. She so, so wished Chris had been nothing more than a blip on her life, that she'd been able to see past the surface before the dice of life rolled and he ended up being much more than a blip. If it weren't for Julianna, Vivi wouldn't even be angry. She wanted to protect Julianna from the pain of loss and of learning she happened to have a father who couldn't even be bothered. When Vivi reached the clearing, the sun was setting on the mountain ridge on the far side of the trees. The sky was a watercolor of soft gold and orange with the last rays of the sun haloing the trees.

Chapter 10

Heath pushed through the door into Mile High Grounds, a gust of wind following him into the coffee shop. It was quiet again since it was late afternoon, his preferred time to stop by. He'd just finished helping Daniel with the last of the window replacements out at the farmhouse and could use a shot of caffeine.

"Hey Heath!" Sophia called out, her voice carrying across the room.

"Hey Soph," he replied as he approached the counter where she waited. "How's it going?"

"Good. Daniel just called and said you guys got the windows all done." Sophia grinned and clapped her hands together softly. "Thank you so much for helping him with that. I don't think we could have moved in this year if you didn't. You made everything happen twice as fast."

Heath shrugged. "No problem. The work's kept me busy while I've been getting a few jobs up and running. Plus, anything for you."

Sophia's grin stretched wider. "It's so awesome your business is actually happening. You know Daniel will help with any projects you need. If you ever get your own house, that is."

"Someday." Vivi immediately came to mind because she was the one and only woman who made him hanker for domesticity. He mentally shook himself. "For now, how about a coffee?"

"Of course, what'll it be today?"

"I'll take a mocha latte today. I could use the caffeine and the sugar."

"Coming right up," Tommy called out from his position behind the espresso machine.

"Do you ever give him a day off?" Heath asked, his eyes bouncing between Tommy and Sophia.

Sophia glared at him. "Of course I do! He only works five days a week. It just so happens you don't bother to show up when he's not here."

"Nah. She works me like a dog," Tommy countered with a grin.

Heath chuckled and leaned against the counter. Sophia turned away and grabbed a towel to wipe down the counter. When she looked back, her eyes had sobered. "Daniel told me about Chris. Have you had a chance to talk to Vivi?"

"Told her last night. She was upset, but she handled it okay. She's mostly upset about how it will affect Julianna."

Sophia twirled the towel between her hands. "It sucks. It's bad enough Julianna barely has a father, but if it turns out Chris is involved with the smuggling network, eventually Vivi will have to explain that to Julianna."

"I know. I wish…"

"Wish what?"

"I just wish Chris wasn't the way he was. Vivi deserves better and Julianna deserves a father who can bother to be around. Has Chris done anything to help since Julianna was born?" Heath thought he knew the answer to this, but he had to know.

Sophia shook her head quickly. "Nothing. He visited a few times for the first couple of years, but that's it. He's never helped take care of her. No child support. Nothing."

A flash of anger rose inside Heath. Every time he thought about Chris, he wanted to pound him in the face and make him pay for what he'd done. This information made him want to use a sledgehammer. "Damn asshole."

Sophia nodded. "Oh yeah. You'll get no argument on that from me. Vivi tries not to dwell, but it's hard with Julianna getting old enough to ask questions."

Tommy stepped to the counter and slid Heath's coffee across. "Here you go. Light on the mocha, just how you like it."

Heath took a taste. "Perfect. Here you go." He tugged his wallet out and a few bills from it before stuffing them in the tip jar.

Tommy grinned, while Sophia rolled her eyes. After Tommy stepped to the back, Sophia caught Heath's eyes again. She appeared to be considering something. Just when Heath was about to ask her what she was thinking, she spoke. "How's it going with Vivi?"

Heath considered last night—another experience with Vivi that nearly brought him to his knees and held her so tight and fast in his heart that he didn't know where to go from here. There were a lot of details he didn't feel comfortable sharing with his sister, but he could use her perspective. "Good, I think. I'm a little worried about what's going on with Chris. For all the obvious reasons, but also because I'm worried she's just gonna get more skittish than she already is."

Sophia picked up a pen on the counter and flipped it back and forth between her fingers. "Probably," she finally said.

"Probably? What does that mean?" Tension coiled within him. He wanted to wipe away the past that marred Vivi's trust, but changing the past was out of his hands.

Sophia grinned. "Exactly that."

"What's so funny?" A slight thread of irritation rose within him. He knew Sophia was only teasing, but Vivi meant too much to him to take anything lightly when it came to her.

Sophia angled her head to the side. "You know, it doesn't surprise me at all to see you fall for Vivi. I guess I didn't realize how impatient you might be."

Heath shook his head and took a gulp of coffee, buying himself a moment to tamp down his annoyance. "I'm not impatient. I just know what I want. Plus, I'd think you'd want me to care how she felt."

"Of course I care!" Her grin faded, and she stopped flipping the pen back and forth. "Julianna is her number one priority. Vivi is going to be skittish about any man because of that. Casual dating isn't exactly easy for single parents. You know and I know you're not going anywhere, but give Vivi a little time to see that for herself."

Heath took another swallow of coffee, savoring the bittersweet flavor, and sighed. "Right. I'll try to be patient. With Chris showing up in the mix around the investigation, I'm just worried, that's all."

***

A while later, Heath walked up the porch steps at Vivi's house. She'd texted and invited him to stop by for dinner. He took that as a remarkably good sign for now. When he reached the door, it flew open and Julianna dashed through it, flinging herself against him in a hug around his legs.

"Heath! Mom said you were coming for dinner again, so I asked her to make crunchy mac and cheese again." Julianna's head was to the side of his hip as she looked up, her brown eyes wide. Her dark hair hung in two long braids down her back. He rested a hand on her back. Her shoulder blades felt like tiny wings when he stroked up and down quickly and leaned over to drop a kiss on her head.

"Really? Well, you know how much I liked it last time. Can't go wrong with that. How are you today?" he asked, giving one of her braids a quick flip as she released his legs and scampered to the porch railing to swing Jax into her arms. Jax wiggled around and settled against her shoulder, instantly starting up his purr.

Julianna spoke over her shoulder as she headed back into the kitchen. "I'm good. I have to finish my homework before dinner though."

Heath followed her inside, a swirl of cool autumn air coming in with them. He closed the door, but not before a leaf skittered across the floor. Jax immediately leapt from Julianna's arms and batted at the leaf. Julianna giggled as Jax subdued the leaf. Vivi caught Heath's eyes with a grin from where she stood by the counter. His heart clenched and heat rolled through him. His lion nearly purred at the sight of her. Her hair was pulled back in a loose ponytail with wisps curling around her face. She wore a pair of cotton pants that hugged her hips and flared to swing around her ankles. As usual, she wore a fitted t-shirt that outlined her breasts. All he had to do was look at her and he was hard. Lust simmered inside. Yet, now was not the time and place to do what he wanted, which was turn her around, bend her over the counter and yank those pants down to plunge inside of her. *Definitely not the time and place, dude. Julianna is about to start her homework. You cannot be thinking like this around her.*

Heath almost laughed aloud when he considered that perhaps he could manage his thoughts, but his body had a mind of its own. When Vivi's eyes met his, it was as if a flame lit the air between them and his body was instantly taut with anticipation. He batted back against those urges and slipped out of his jacket to hang it up on the coatrack by the door before walking over to the kitchen table where Julianna was pulling out a folder. When Vivi's voice reached him, he realized he was so entranced with her, he hadn't even bothered to say hello.

"Hey there, glad you could make it for dinner."

He sat down in the chair facing Vivi and glanced up, feeling foolish. "Wouldn't have missed it. Thanks for having me. How was your day?"

Vivi lifted one shoulder in a soft shrug. "Busy with work. How about you?"

"Daniel and I finished up the window replacements at the farmhouse today. Nothing else new."

Vivi nodded and turned away to fill a pot with water. When she moved to set it one the stove, he noticed her favoring one side. Julianna distracted him at that moment when she slipped into the chair beside him. "Heath, can you help me with this?"

He glanced over to see a math worksheet. He looked back to Vivi, uncertain if she'd want him to help Julianna with her homework. Vivi glanced over her shoulder and nodded. "Help all you want." She turned back and pulled out the baking tray and started grating cheese.

Heath pulled his chair over beside Julianna and looked down at her worksheet. Not much later, after Julianna agonized over several division problems, she carefully returned her homework to its folder and put her backpack away on the bench by the door. Heath leaned back in his chair and looked up to find Vivi's eyes on him. She was standing by the stove. Her eyes reached in and grabbed ahold of his heart. *This* is what he wanted every night—to feel like their lives were entwined together.

When Julianna raced out of the kitchen and into the bathroom, Heath stood from the table and walked to Vivi's side. He quickly dipped his head and dropped a kiss in the curve of her neck. Her breath drew in sharply, and his cock hardened instantly. "Nice to see you," he mumbled into her neck.

He lifted his head and stepped back, knowing he couldn't trust himself if he stayed that close. The mere scent of her pulled on the leash of his control. Her eyes were on his the moment he lifted his head. "Nice to see you too," she said softly. The oven beeped, breaking through the moment. Vivi lifted the tray of macaroni and cheese. "Can you get the oven for me?" she asked, glancing to him.

He quickly reached over to open it. She slid the tray in, and he closed the oven door. The sound of Julianna's footsteps reached them. She came skidding back into the kitchen, dragging a loose string of yarn behind her on the floor. Jax was at her heels, pouncing and batting at the yarn.

***

Vivi closed the dishwasher and snagged a towel to wipe down the counter. Heath had helped Julianna put the dishes in the dishwasher and tidy the table. Julianna had picked up Jax's favorite piece of yarn again and was seated on the floor, dragging it in slow circles while he chased it.

"Time to get ready for bed," Vivi called out to Julianna.

Julianna glanced up, her mouth tightening. "But

Mom, Heath's here! Can't I stay up a little late?"

Vivi shook her head firmly. "It's a school night, and we already talked about this. The deal was Heath could come to dinner as long as you still went to bed on time. We started dinner late as it is, so you need to hop to it. Bed by eight-fifteen."

Julianna gave a drawn out sigh, but she climbed to her feet and slowly walked to the bathroom. Heath glanced over from where he was sitting at the table and grinned. "I always hated bedtime."

Vivi laughed softly. "Didn't we all? Most of the time, she's pretty good about it. She's never thrilled, but she goes along. If anyone's over though, she tends to whine a bit. I've gotten better about reminding her beforehand. Honestly, I can't complain." She gestured toward the bathroom door where they could hear water running. "She's already in there brushing her teeth. She'll probably look pretty pathetic when she comes out to say goodnight though, so be prepared."

He chuckled and leaned back in his chair. "You're a damn good mother."

She flushed. Ever since the day she'd held Julianna in her arms, she felt like she was flying blind half the time. She worried she was too easygoing some days and too strict on others. When Julianna butted heads with her teacher last year, she'd felt so small when she went in to talk to the school. Her tendency to bluster her way through things didn't seem like the smart approach to dealing with the school, so she'd had to find a way to make it work. Now that Julianna was getting older, Vivi felt like she must've done some things right because Julianna was a pretty good kid for the most part. When she glanced over at Heath, she felt like she could see the wheels turning in his head.

"What?" she asked, feeling self-conscious.

He was quiet for a few beats and drummed his fingertips on the table. "Seems like this probably hasn't been the easiest thing for you. Raising Julianna on your own, I mean."

Vivi hung the towel over the oven door handle and leaned against the counter. "Well…no. I wouldn't trade it for a second, but I had no idea how hard it could be."

He nodded slowly and the tapping of his fingertips stopped. "I'm sorry you had to do it alone."

His words were gruff. She wasn't sure how to respond, but she felt she should say something. "It is what it is." She started to push away from the counter, moving a little too quickly, and flinched at the soreness from the deep scratch on her shoulder.

Heath's eyes narrowed. "Are you okay?"

"Yeah, yeah, I'm fine," she replied quickly.

Just then, the bathroom door opened and Julianna came out. "All done!" She hurried through the living room into the kitchen and ran to Vivi's side. "Can I please stay up a little bit longer?" She tugged on Vivi's arm, causing another shot of pain to zip through Vivi's shoulder.

Before Vivi had a chance to answer, Heath spoke. "Remember what your mom said?"

Julianna loosened her hold on Vivi's arm. Vivi breathed a sigh of relief. The scratch from her fight with Chris was deep and happened to land on the curve of her shoulder, so the wrong motion sent pain shooting through the torn skin.

Julianna took a few steps to the center of the kitchen, idly twisting the edge of her t-shirt in her fingers. She chewed her lip. "She said we had a deal," Julianna said in her singsong voice.

Vivi could see Heath was fighting a smile. He kept his expression carefully controlled. "What was the deal?"

"That if you came to dinner, I'd go to bed on time," Julianna answered softly.

Heath nodded slowly. "So?"

Julianna sighed and dropped the edge of her t-shirt. "Okay. I'll go to bed."

Vivi bit her lip to keep from laughing at Julianna's dejected face. She stepped away from the counter and knelt down at Julianna's side, sliding her hands down her arms. "G'night, sweetie. Don't forget to put your clothes in your hamper."

Julianna leaned forward and plopped a noisy kiss on Vivi's cheek before hurrying to the table to throw her arms around Heath's waist. He hugged her to his side.

Julianna tilted her face up to him. "Can you come for dinner again soon?"

"All you have to do is tell your mom to ask me and I'll be here. Now off to bed. Night, night."

Julianna giggled and scampered off. Once her bedroom door closed, Heath stood from the table.

"Okay, what happened?" he asked.

"What do you mean?" Vivi hedged. She sensed he noticed she was favoring her shoulder, but she'd prefer not to explain.

"You're moving like you got hurt. Did you overdue it at work, or something?" He lifted a hand to curl over her shoulder. She managed not to flinch, but she tensed.

His eyes canted down, and he hooked his thumb over the edge of her shirt and pushed it back, slowly revealing her shoulder. He stopped when the ragged edge of the deep scratch came into view. His eyes bounced back up to hers. He repeated his question. "Vivi, what happened?"

She shrugged, feeling annoyed and defensive. "I went out to look for Chris." Her heart pounded wildly against her ribs. Having Heath this close sent her body into a tailspin. The air felt loaded—with desire, with the longing to lean into him and let him take care of her.

"I take it you found him," Heath said softly, his voice low and taut.

She nodded and swallowed. "I did. I just had to know if it was him."

"How the hell did you get this? Please don't tell me he went after you. Because if he did, I'll fucking kill him."

"I chased after him. I was so pissed. I just... I don't know. . Finding out Chris was involved just made me sick. I had to know for sure, so I went out there. I chased him and went after him. He fought back, but he bolted once he pinned me. I know he's a total ass, but if he really wanted to hurt me, he could've. He had me pinned."

She couldn't quite believe she was defending Chris, but she believed what she was saying. Chris hadn't set out to hurt her. He fought back. The minute he had a chance to do real damage, he bolted. She didn't know what was going to come of everything, but Heath going after Chris to avenge an injury she sustained from a fight she started didn't seem like it would do anything other than make things even messier. In hindsight, she wished she'd told the police she was going out there, so they could have followed her and brought Chris in.

Heath traced the edge of the scratch, his index finger drawing alongside it. He stopped before the fabric of her shirt pulled too much. His breath drew in sharply. She lifted her eyes again and collided with his. "Why didn't you tell me you wanted to go find him?"

"Because I knew you'd tell me not to go." A thread of stubbornness rose within her. While one part of her wanted to lean into the protectiveness and shelter Heath offered, another part of her wanted to push against it. She'd been independent for so long, it was hard to let herself rely on anyone. She'd also needed to confront Chris, to try to allay her lingering anger.

He held her gaze, his eyes considering. "I might have wanted to tell you not to go, but I would've understood why you wanted to. I just wish you'd told me so I could've gone with you. That's all." He paused and took a deep breath. "And I'm fucking pissed he hurt you."

Warmth curled around her heart. Even if it was unfamiliar and she wasn't quite sure how to handle it, part of her savored his protectiveness and willingness to fight for her. He eased his hand off of her shoulder and carefully adjusted her t-shirt. The room was quiet. The fall wind blowing outside gusted against the windows. The air around them came to life. Vivi's breath became shallow and hot need rolled through her. She scrambled to hold it at bay. Now was not the time to tackle Heath. Julianna was probably still awake, reading in her room, and Vivi had promised herself no matter what happened with Heath, she would keep it contained from Julianna.

Heath's hand stroked down her back, sending prickles up her spine and over her skin. He dipped his head to rest against her shoulder. She couldn't resist sliding a hand up his muscled back and into his curls. He lifted his head, his eyes locking onto hers. "Let me…" he said gruffly before his lips caught hers.

What started as a soft kiss exploded within seconds. His tongue swept inside, stroking against hers, before he drew back and traced her lips. He dove in for another fierce kiss, leaving her gasping for air when he tore his lips free of hers and trailed wet kisses down the column of her neck. Hot shivers chased in the wake of his touch. She felt the heat of his palm like a brand where it rested in the dip of her waist. His lips reached the juncture of her shoulder when he stilled and slowly lifted his head. She could feel his hard shaft in the cradle of her hips, which arched into him of their own accord. A hot flush raced up her cheeks when his hand slid down to cup her bottom and pulled her tight against him. A shock of pleasure jolted her when his knee slid between her thighs, exerting a subtle pressure against the very place she wanted him most. With not much more than a kiss, he'd sent need spinning through her and left her drenched with want.

She took a shuddering breath and lifted her eyes. "Um…maybe…"

"I should go," he said softly, finishing what she was about to say.

She bit her lip. "I don't want you to go," she whispered. As soon as the words left her mouth, she couldn't believe she'd said them. It was that bad. Heath was, well, he was Heath. With things unfolding with him, it was near impossible to hold back from what she wanted.

"And I don't want to go, but I'm not thinking it's the best plan for me to do what I want to do with Julianna's bedroom light still on." He angled his head in the direction of her bedroom. A thin strip of light was bright under the door.

Vivi grinned. "She likes to read for a little bit before she falls asleep. I don't fight her on it."

Heath took a step back. Her entire body pulled toward him. She had to fight to hold herself back from tugging him right back against her. He watched her for a moment before turning to take a few steps to the coatrack. He snagged his coat off of it and shrugged into it. He returned to her and dipped his head for a quick kiss. "I'm only leaving now because if I stay for much longer, I won't be able to stop myself. Don't suppose you'll let me know next time you have a shift at Quinn's?"

"Tomorrow night," she said quickly, desperate to

J.H. Croix

see him again as soon as possible.

His mouth hitched at one corner. "I'll give you a ride home." His gravelly words sent a shiver through her.

Julianna would be with her mother tomorrow night, so Vivi wouldn't have to shackle the need coursing through her. She nodded. "Okay. See you then."

At that, he turned and quietly opened the door. When it clicked shut behind him, Vivi waited as she heard him walk down the porch stairs. At the sound of his truck starting, she locked the door, hugged her arms around her waist and walked through the living room toward her bedroom. She paused by Julianna's door. "Lights out soon," she called out softly.

When she didn't hear a response, she carefully turned the doorknob and peeked around the door. Julianna was sound asleep with her book on her chest. Vivi stepped quietly into her room and placed the book on her nightstand before clicking the lamp off and tiptoeing out of the room. Vivi climbed into her own bed, the sheets cool against her skin. She had trouble falling asleep, her mind spinning over thoughts of Heath and her body still humming from their kiss.

Chapter 11

Heath leaned against the railing on the porch at Daniel's farmhouse and glanced around while he waited for Daniel. They were meeting to head out and scout for Chris. Every time he thought about the fact that Vivi went out to find him on her own, he swung between fear and anger. She was okay, but it infuriated him Chris had injured her. The sky was overcast this morning and the air held a bite to it. They were well into autumn with winter nipping at its heels. Daniel came out of the front door and took a few strides to sit on the front steps beside where Heath was waiting.

Daniel stared out into the trees before turning in Heath's direction. "So did you get more details from Vivi about where she saw Chris?"

Heath nodded. "Yeah. Called her this morning. She told me she headed toward the caves along the ridge out that way. Those are a few miles from the old logging road. Shouldn't take us long. I'm worried he may be on the move, but if we start there, we should be able to pick up his scent." He paused and shook his head. "I'm still pissed she went out on her own."

"Don't blame you, but I see why she wanted to. How bad did he get her?"

"All in all, not bad. I only saw part of the scratch, but it's an angry slash on her shoulder. She thinks he was fighting defensively because she started it. Based on how she described it, he could have done a lot worse but he took off. Doesn't matter to me whether she started it or not, if we find him, he'll wish he hadn't touched her." Heath's lion simmered under his skin. He hoped he had enough control to keep from killing Chris. He pushed away from the railing. "Let's go."

A while later, he and Daniel were weaving their way through the trees. Power coursed through Heath in surges. His anger toward Chris was amped once he shifted with primal instinct and drive taking over. They ascended steadily into the mountains, the ground becoming rockier as they made their way up. They reached the area where Vivi had told him she'd encountered Chris. Evidence of recent activity was present, along with Chris's scent. Heath was slightly surprised at the strength of the scent. It indicated Chris had been in the area within hours. He and Daniel had agreed they would hang close to each other, keeping within sight and sound at all times. The point of today was to bring Chris in, so they needed to be able to easily subdue him if they found him.

They scoured the area around the boulders and caves in the rocky cliff before following Chris's scent. They initially climbed higher into the mountains where the trees began to thin out, but the trail of his scent looped down, leading back toward the old logging road. A soft rain began to fall. A short while later, a motion in the distance caught Heath's eyes. He froze, Daniel abruptly stopping at his side. Through the trees, they could see an old shed, likely built years ago to store tools for the loggers when they were working in the area. A man stood beside it, smoking a cigarette. Heath couldn't tell from sight that it was Chris, but he recognized his scent from the other day. He swung his head to the side, indicating he would loop around and approach the shed from the far side. Daniel would wait here to close in from this side.

Heath's lion was rumbling to let loose, but he forced himself to maintain control. He didn't want Chris to get away today, so he had to keep his anger in check. What he wanted to do was bolt straight for him and take him down. Instead, he moved stealthily through the trees, his fur dampening from the rain falling steadily now. Once he got to the far side of the shed, he zigzagged through the trees. He could see Daniel slowly approaching from the other side. He was surprised Chris hadn't sensed their presence yet, although the cigarette smoke likely obscured their scent. A few more seconds and he was close enough. Chris turned his head.

Heath leapt through the trees with a low growl. Chris shifted instantly, his cigarette falling to the ground and snuffing out in the rain. The next few moments were a tangled mess of claws and snarls. Daniel closed in, but he held back. Heath knew Daniel was giving him the chance to take Chris down on his own because that's what his lion needed. Chris was a strong cat, but an untrained fighter. Heath had years of fighting in lion form on his side, along with years of military training that honed him into top condition. It had only been recently he'd regained his full strength after the accident, but now energy and adrenaline pulsed through in waves of pure power.

Chris fought defensively, backing up into the trees and leaping into branches to dodge. Heath followed him onto a sturdy pine branch and backed Chris against the tree, snarling and growling. Chris tumbled off the branch with Heath following. He took advantage of Chris's shaky balance and knocked him off his feet, pinning him. With Chris struggling mightily under him, Heath bit into his neck, the taste of iron seeping into his mouth. He held on, shaking his head slightly when Chris tried to resist until Chris's body relaxed under him. Heath kept seeing Vivi flinch in his mind, that subtle reminder of the small damage Chris had inflicted on her. With anger pounding through him, he kept a firm grip on his human mind to keep from tearing Chris's throat out.

Daniel approached and waited at Heath's side as he slowly eased his grip on Chris's throat. Heath's breath misted in the cool, rainy air of the forest.

***

Vivi leaned against the counter at Mile High Grounds and reached out to curl her hand around the cup of coffee Sophia slid across.

"There you go. House coffee with a shot of espresso," Sophia said with a grin.

Vivi took a welcome sip and sighed. "Oh God, that's so good. I can't get warm today. I'm like that whenever it's rainy in the fall."

"Me too," Sophia replied as she twirled her hair into a knot and stuck a pen through it. Her hands fell to the counter and she angled her head to the side. "So how come you didn't bother to tell anyone you went off to look for Chris?"

Vivi sighed, feeling defensive and annoyed. "Look, I just needed to know it was him. I wasn't out there to take him down or bring him in. I know I should've said something…"

Sophia cut in. "Yes! You should have." She nodded

her head vigorously for emphasis. "We agreed last year we wouldn't go out alone like that. Maybe you didn't want to involve Heath, but you could've at least told me. You know I'd have gone with you. You're damn lucky you didn't get hurt worse."

Vivi took another sip of coffee, savoring the warmth and flavor. Guilt pulsed through her. She knew she'd be pissed if the situation were reversed. She hadn't been thinking too clearly when she'd gone out to find Chris. She'd been afraid anyone she mentioned it to would tell her not to go, so she'd kept it to herself. She looked into Sophia's concerned gaze and shrugged. "I'm sorry. I should've told you. I got all worked up in my head and just had to find out if it was really him. I didn't think he would hurt me. I know Heath's pissed about it, but honestly Chris didn't start the fight. I did. Sure, he fought back and pinned me, but even though he had a chance to do worse, he took off."

"Oh, so now he's a good guy?" Sophia said with a roll of her eyes.

Vivi returned the eye roll and shook her head. "No. He's most definitely not a good guy. He's Julianna's asshole father who can't be bothered and is so stupid he got involved in the smuggling network. He's all of that and then some, but I don't want to make things worse by acting like he was out to hurt me. I don't believe he was. If he wanted to, he could have. Instead, he bolted."

Sophia's eyes softened. "I get it. I just hate that you put yourself in that position."

"Maybe it wasn't my smartest move, but I'm fine. Let's hope Daniel and Heath find him and bring him in today. Maybe we'll get more info on where the hell Nelson is these days."

"Let's hope so." Sophia paused to take another

customer's order.

After the customer stepped away while Tommy prepped the coffee, Sophia looked to Vivi again. "Heath was pretty upset about what happened."

Vivi's chest tightened, her heart almost aching. It was hard to think about how much Heath was coming to mean to her. She nodded quickly. "I know." Vivi could feel Sophia's assessing gaze on her.

"Do you know how he feels about you?"

Vivi shrugged, uncertain how to answer.

Sophia paused again and slid the coffee Tommy passed to her over the counter to the customer. Once the woman picked it up and walked away, Sophia turned her way too perceptive gaze back on Vivi. "You're it for him," she said bluntly.

Vivi's heart gave a swift kick. Sophia's blunt point should have made her want to dance for joy. Part of her did, yet another part couldn't quite believe it and had no idea how to assimilate the idea of Heath into her life in the concrete sense. She felt Sophia's watchful gaze on her and looked up. She didn't even realize she was chewing on the inside of her mouth until Sophia started to smile slowly.

Vivi sighed. "I don't know what to do."

Sophia called to Tommy over her shoulder. "Coffee break for me!" She snagged a cup of coffee, slipped from behind the counter and hooked her hand through Vivi's elbow, tugging her to a nearby table in the corner. Vivi dropped into the chair across from Sophia at the tiny round table. Sophia leaned her elbows on the table. "You are seriously stressing out."

Vivi took a gulp of coffee and leaned back in her chair. "Pretty much. I'm just… Ugh." She waved a hand in the air. "I don't know how to handle this thing with Heath. It's not that I don't want it. I do, I really do. But it's got me spinning circles in my head. I keep worrying about how to handle things with Julianna. I mean, I haven't even dated anyone since Chris. Now with him surfacing again, it's even more confusing."

"Only if you make it that way," Sophia countered.

Vivi picked up a packet of sugar from the holder on the table and twirled it between her fingers. "You make it sound easy, like I'll just decide it's not complicated and it won't be."

Sophia sighed rather dramatically and rolled her eyes for good measure. "I'm not pretending like it's a piece of cake. As far as bringing a man into your life with Julianna, Heath makes it so much easier. Julianna adores him and you know he will always put her first. You don't have to worry about him leaving you high and dry. Heath doesn't do anything halfway. I'm not so sure why you two didn't figure it out sooner, but you're perfect for each other." Sophia paused and angled her head to the side. "You have plenty of reasons to be protective of yourself and of Julianna, but you don't need to worry with Heath. With Chris showing up, well, maybe it's better to rip that scab off."

Vivi absorbed what Sophia said, the wheels in her mind starting to slow. She was struggling to accept how simple it sounded from Sophia. Yet, she knew Sophia was right about one thing—Heath was loyal. Unlike Chris, he wouldn't just up and leave. She took a quick sip of coffee and felt some of the tension ease from her shoulders. "I hear you, I do. It's just… I don't know. Maybe you'd understand if you knew I had a thing for Heath way back when we were in high school."

"You think I never noticed that?" Sophia countered with a grin.

"You did not!"

"Maybe I wasn't sure how bad you had it for him, but I noticed. Just like I noticed he kind of had a thing for you. I'm not stupid though, so I decided it was best to keep myself out of the middle. I figured it would blow over, and it did. Until he came back last year. Now, here we are."

Vivi's cheeks got hot. She grinned ruefully. "Fine then. So I had a thing for him. It just makes it harder because if things go south…"

Sophia threw her hands up. "Did it ever occur to you that it's not really helpful to assume the worst? You had one guy treat you like shit, but Chris is just that—one guy. If it wasn't for Julianna, I doubt you'd even dwell on it. Not to mention that you know Heath believes you're his mate. Don't lecture me on that being a bunch of bullshit because you were all about it with me and Daniel."

Vivi finished off her coffee and sighed, recalling how she'd encouraged Sophia to believe in what she felt for Daniel. It all seemed so much simpler when it wasn't her own heart on the line. She bit her lip and wrinkled her nose. "Fine. I'll try to be more optimistic. Maybe that'll be easier after we get Chris in and I can close the book on him."

Chapter 12

Heath leaned against the wall in Roger's office and rolled his head to the side when Daniel spoke.

"You can hold him then?" Daniel asked Roger.

Roger nodded. "Oh yeah. With the stash of drugs stuffed in that old shed, we can hold him on possession charges with intent to distribute. I figure we'll let him stew for the night and try to question him again in the morning." His eyes glanced from Daniel to Heath. "Gotta say, I was hopeful you two might have a bit more luck than us, but you brought him in quicker than I expected. I'm thinking he got rattled by his little spat with Vivi, just enough to throw him off his game."

A curl of anger rose within Heath. He'd gotten plenty of it out of his system in the fight earlier, but it still burned. He shoved it away and nodded tightly. "Just relieved he's here now. I'm hoping he can give us a few clues on where Nelson might be lying low."

"I have a feeling he will. Nelson doesn't have too many shifters left willing to help him. Chris is also most worried about himself. If we offer him some concessions to talk, he probably will. It'll just take him a little time to realize Nelson can't do him much good anymore."

Heath pushed away from the wall. "Right. Well, let us know when you have an update." He glanced to Daniel. "You ready to go? I could seriously use a shower."

Daniel grinned and stood from where he'd been half-sitting on a file cabinet. "You and me both. Let's go."

A while later, Heath drove back toward downtown Painter after dropping Daniel off at the farmhouse. As he drove along Main Street, he recalled he was supposed to meet Vivi at Quinn's at the end of her shift. He raced home, showered in record time and started to walk out the door. He forgot his keys and turned back to snag them off the kitchen counter. He paused and looked around his small apartment. In the aftermath of his accident, he'd stayed with his parents for a while since he had only planned to be home for a few weeks and didn't have a place of his own. Once he finally cobbled his life back together after the accident, he'd needed his own place.

Yet, the place he 'lived' was barely lived in. The living room and kitchen had the requisite furniture basics, but he'd never gotten around to decorating and rarely spent time here. The space felt stark and bare. His mind flashed to the way Vivi's home felt—warm and inviting, so comfortable it was like stepping into a favorite pair of slippers. At the thought of Vivi, his body kicked into gear and he swung away, his keys in hand.

***

Vivi flew around behind the bar, taking orders, making drinks and swiping bills for payment. Quinn's was filled to the brim tonight, its usual state. Even though she barely had time to stop and think, her eyes kept wandering toward the door, wondering when Heath would arrive. He'd called her earlier to let her know they'd brought Chris in. While she had plenty of questions about Chris, her thoughts were honed in on Heath. Between her conversation with Sophia today and her unsatisfied desire last night, Heath was like a fever in her brain. She swung on the pendulum of her hopes. At times, she could almost convince herself she could try to believe it might work out with him, while at others, her doubts scoffed at the idea.

"Viv, can you pass me another pint of the house beer?" Dan asked from the far end of the bar.

She turned quickly, snagged a pint glass and filled it swiftly. She glanced to Dan, and he nodded in the direction of the customer in question. She slid the beer down the counter. "There you go!" The guy caught it with a grin and immediately tipped his head back for a gulp.

Dan called out a quick thanks, holding two bottles of liquor in his hands as he made two drinks at once. Another customer called her name and she swung away to make another drink. Another half hour rolled by and she spun around to grab a towel to wipe up a spill.

"Hey Vivi."

Her eyes flew up from the counter and collided with Heath's. He'd snagged the barstool against the wall again. His green gaze caught hers and her low belly clenched, flutters twirling madly inside. Heat flashed through her and her breath hitched when his mouth stretched into a slow smile.

"Hey," she managed. "I was wondering if you were still going to make it tonight."

"Never any question I'd be here," he replied, his eyes dark and intent.

"I just wondered if you were tired after everything that happened today."

He lifted a shoulder in a half-shrug. "Busy day, but

all I wanted was to see you," he said bluntly.

Another wash of heat raced through her. She was so distracted by him, she jumped when Dan tapped her on the shoulder from behind. When she turned, Dan was chuckling. "Just letting you know you can head home if you want."

Vivi glanced to the clock above the door into the back. "But I've still got an hour left and it's nuts here."

Dan shrugged. "Danny just showed up. He'll help us close out." Danny was Dan's son who'd recently moved back to Painter and started helping out at the bar here and there.

Normally, Vivi wouldn't want to miss out on an hour's worth of tips. On a night like tonight, that could be good money. Yet, all she could think about was how soon she could be alone with Heath. "If you're sure."

Dan's eyes canted from her to Heath. "I'm sure. Get out of here. See you at your next shift."

Vivi untied her apron and pushed through the swinging door into the back. Minutes later, she met Heath at the front door. The streetlights were glittering in the cold air when they stepped outside. Some autumn evenings hinted at the winter to come and tonight was one of those. Heath's palm stroked down her back. She could feel the heat of it through her jacket, electricity prickling along her spine.

While Heath maneuvered his truck on the short drive from Main Street to her house, he kept one hand on the steering wheel and the other curled over her thigh. His thumb stroked in slow circles on the inside of her thigh. By the time he pulled up at her house, longing held her in its grip. All she wanted was him.

When they walked through the back door into the kitchen, she took a shaky breath as she shrugged out of her jacket and kicked her shoes off. Restless, she walked through the kitchen into the living room. Heath followed her after he hung up his own jacket and left his boots by the door. She stopped by the couch, struggling to contain the wild feeling inside of her. When she lifted her eyes and saw his answering desire, an electric current sparked to life between them. The space around them compressed—charged with desire. He stood a few feet away and swiftly closed the distance. With no hesitation, he tugged her roughly against him and caught her lips in a fierce kiss. The tinder of desire inside ignited as their kiss went wild—a tangle of lips, tongue and teeth.

She couldn't get close enough fast enough and yanked at his clothing. All she wanted was to be skin to skin with him, as close as physically possible. He tore his lips free and reached behind his neck to pull his shirt off when her hands traveled up his chest. He took another step back to unbutton her blouse, while she tugged his jeans open. His breath drew in sharply when she slipped her hand into his briefs and stroked his cock. Next thing she knew, he yanked at the last few buttons and tossed her shirt free with her bra following immediately. His lips closed around a nipple, taut and tight. While he licked, sucked and nipped at her breasts, his hands were busy at her jeans. In seconds, he'd shoved them down around her hips and stroked a finger across her damp cotton panties. She was drenched with need, her channel convulsing at the mere hint of what was to come.

Need spun her in its grip, pushing her to a wildness inside she could hardly tolerate. All she knew was she needed more and now. She shoved his jeans and briefs to the floor. His cock sprang free, and she immediately leaned forward and dragged her tongue along the underside.

"Vivi."

Heath said her name roughly. As she lifted her eyes, he shoved her jeans off with her panties following. She kicked them free. He lifted her in his arms and turned to sit on the couch, settling her on his lap. She almost came right then and there when he arched into her, the hot, hard length of his shaft rubbing between her slick folds and teasing her clit. He cupped her breasts and dragged his thumbs across her nipples, still moist from his touch. He freed one breast and stroked his hand down over the curve of her belly and dipped into her curls. With one hand teasing her nipple and his other circling over her clit, her breath came in raw gasps. She heard his name fall from her lips—rough, broken and pleading for more.

Spikes of pleasure shot through her. Her hips rolled against him as she chased after release. He suddenly paused, his hand curling over her hip to hold her still. His fingers dug into her skin. Disoriented and almost bereft at the brief interruption, she dragged her eyes open.

"I need to grab a condom. Let me…"

She shook her head. "We don't need one. I'm on the pill." When he hesitated, she felt suddenly embarrassed, uncertain if he felt the way she did. All she knew was she trusted him completely and only wanted to be as close as possible with no barriers. Something must have shown on her face because he eased his grip on her hip and stroked his palm up her back to thread into her hair. Hot shivers chased along her spine on the heels of his touch.

"Okay," he said, so softly she almost didn't hear him.

The anxious uncertainty that had started to build eased inside. She was coiled so tight with need she thought she might explode. He shifted his hips slightly and reached between them. She lifted her hips. Just when she thought she'd sink onto him, he dragged the head of his cock back and forth through the wet folds. Heat flooded through her, feverish need holding her in its grip. He freed his hand from her hair and brought it down to curl on her hip again, slowly bringing her down onto him as he surged inside of her.

She moaned, her head falling into the dip of his shoulder when he started to move. The delicious stretch of him deepened with each roll of his hips meeting hers. Tremors began to build inside, pressure gathering as he thrust into her again and again and again. A rush of bliss raced through her. She was flying and he flew with her, their cries mingling as they shuddered against each other.

She slowly drifted down, her body easing into his hold. She rested in his arms, his skin warm against hers. She didn't want to move because she finally felt at ease, twined together with him. His hand stroked through her hair, brushing it back from her face. When she finally lifted her head, she found him waiting for her, his eyes intent and dark. The rush of intimacy was so pure, she couldn't look away.

***

Heath leaned against the headboard and watched Vivi. She was walking out of the bathroom adjacent to her bedroom. Her dark hair hung in damp waves around her shoulders. She was idly untangling a section of it when she glanced up to see him watching her. A subtle flush crested her cheekbones. She climbed onto the bed beside him, crossing her legs and flipping the covers over her lap. After they'd untwined themselves from each other earlier, they'd showered together and she'd headed to the kitchen, returning with a bowl of popcorn and two glasses of wine.

She leaned against the headboard beside him and grabbed the remote off of her nightstand. "Your pick. Star

Trek reruns or Simpsons reruns?"

"Those are my only choices?" he teased. He knew
she was a big fan of both because of the number of
overnight slumber parties she had with Sophia when they
were in high school. Those were the days when he
studiously avoided spending too much time with her
because it just wasn't kosher for him to lust after his little
sister's best friend. Back then, the three years between
them seemed huge, a barrier he couldn't have considered
crossing. Now, at thirty-two, three years between them
seemed like nothing.

Vivi took a bite of popcorn out of the bowl she'd set
on the bed beside him a few minutes ago. She glanced
sideways with a grin. "Yup, those are your choices. What'll
it be?"

"Let's go with Simpsons. I'm not sure how long I'll
be able to stay awake. It's been a long day."

Her grin widened as she flicked the television on
and quickly selected the channel. The cheery Simpsons
theme started up as he reached into the bowl and swiped a
handful of popcorn.

After a few minutes, Vivi's spoke. "You look a little
banged up from today."

Heath rolled his head to the side to find her blue
eyes on him, concern held in their depths. He nodded. "I
took a few bumps and bruises. Nothing to worry about."

She chewed on another bite of popcorn and
swallowed. "I was worried about you today," she said, so
softly he could barely hear her words.

Her eyes canted down, and she appeared suddenly
interested in the pattern on her quilt as she traced along the
edges of one of the downy squares.

"I'm okay," he said, his throat tight with emotion.
Something about her quiet words hit him right in the heart.

Vivi was so strong and so well-guarded, he knew how much it took for her to say aloud she'd been worried. He also knew if he commented on it, she'd likely retreat. Instead, he slid his hand over the covers to curl over her thigh and gave her a soft squeeze.

She looked up again, her eyes bright with moisture. "I think I might understand a little better why you were so upset when I went after Chris on my own." She shook her head sharply and emitted a small laugh. "I didn't think about how it might feel for you."

"Fair enough. So maybe next time you'll let me know if you decide to do something like that?"

She lifted a shoulder and let it fall. "I would, but it's not like it will matter much anymore. Aside from tracking down Nelson, there aren't a whole lot of reasons I'd head out on my own like that. Don't go worrying I plan to try to track him either! I figure that's up to the police and you and Daniel. I've had my fill of scouting."

He chuckled. "Good to know. How's your shoulder by the way?"

"It's fine. Just a little sore." She reached for another handful of popcorn.

"You planning to try to talk to Chris?" He couldn't help but ask even though he thought he knew the answer. Vivi needed to clear the air with Chris with regard to Julianna. Heath only hoped that might knock down some of the hurdles between him and Vivi. She might be letting him in, but he didn't doubt they had a ways to go when it came to Julianna. He'd never dated a single mother. Frankly, he hadn't dated much period. With so much travel during his career in the military, he hadn't had time for much other than brief, casual relationships. He had enough sense to know Vivi would want to be certain about them before she allowed Julianna to see him as anything other than how she currently did.

Vivi finally answered, her words clear and calm. "I do. I need to finally say what I've wanted to say for a while about how he's treated Julianna. I'm hoping he can man up enough to be honest with me. Separate from his legal problems, I'd like to know if he ever plans to try to connect with her. If not, that's fine. Well, it sucks, but it's fine because he hasn't yet. Julianna has questions and I'd prefer to be honest with her. I'm not going to bash him, but if he doesn't plan to be around, it would be good if he could just say that. Up to now, it's just what's happened."

She glanced sideways. "What do you think?"

Heath was startled she wanted his opinion, but it warmed him and gave him a strong glimmer of hope he might mean as much to her as she did to him. "I think you should talk to him. No matter what I think of him, he's Julianna's father. It's best for her if you have an idea if he plans to try to be around or not. If not, you can help her find a way to accept that."

Vivi held his gaze for several beats before nodding firmly. "Exactly." At that, she leaned back, grabbed another handful of popcorn and turned toward the television. A while later, the room was quiet save for Jax's unbelievably loud purr emanating from the foot of the bed. Vivi was curled against him with one of her legs thrown over his. Her breathing was soft and even. Inside, he started to unwind and drifted into sleep.

Chapter 13

Vivi pushed through the door of Mile High Grounds out into the chilly autumn morning. She and Heath had stopped here for coffee this morning. He'd headed out a few minutes ahead of her for a meeting on a new job. He was putting together the blueprints for a housing complex. He wouldn't start building until next spring, but the planning was on track. She took a sip of coffee and crossed the street to her car. She rarely drove into town, but today she was going to one of her regular jobs to prep their flowerbeds before winter set in and plant a few more perennials. Although spring was the growing season, autumn was the planting season in her world. Autumn was when it was time to prepare for what would come out of the ground after the snow melted. She planned to stop by the jail this afternoon and try to talk with Chris.

A few hours later, she knocked the dirt loose from her work gloves and kicked her boots against her tire. She rested her fists on her hips and surveyed the yard. It was ready for winter. She'd planted some more daffodil bulbs in the front of the house and mulched all of the flowerbeds.

After tucking her tools away, she scribbled a note for the owners that she'd mail the bill and took off. Her next stop was the jail. Every time she thought about coming face to face with Chris after all this time and after their rough encounter in the mountains the other day, her stomach clenched. She was determined to have this out with him, but it didn't mean she was looking forward to it.

When she arrived at the police station, she checked in with Roger first. "Any updates?" she asked, a question she felt like she'd asked hundreds of times ever since she and Sophia got involved with the investigation into the smuggling network last year.

Roger leaned back in his chair and ran a hand through his dark hair. "Not a ton, but we did get some new info from Chris. He was stubborn at first, but after he met with his public defender, seems like he decided he'd be better off if he tried to make a deal to reduce his charges."

Vivi plunked down in the chair across from Roger's desk. "Well?"

"Chris swears he only started working for Nelson about a year ago. I doubt that part of his story, but he's trying to minimize the fallout for himself. What the other guy we're holding told us is consistent with Chris's version of his involvement. Chris was handling deliveries. He claims he didn't transport himself, but my gut tells me he did. More risk and more money. Since Nelson slipped away, Chris says he's been hiding out in various locations. He swears he doesn't know where Nelson is right now. I buy that because Nelson isn't going to risk letting someone know where he is. Even if he trusts Chris to try to get his back, it's safer for him if no one knows his whereabouts. If they don't know, they can't give it away by accident." Roger paused to take a swig of coffee from a battered paper cup.

"So how does any of this help us?" Vivi asked, frustrated that it didn't sound like Chris had much to offer that they couldn't have guessed.

Roger set his coffee cup down and leaned his elbows on the desk. "Let me finish before you get too impatient with me. I bet you're thinking you could have guessed all this. Sure, we all could've. But it doesn't mean it's not helpful to actually confirm a few things. Having Chris in custody cuts off another source of support for Nelson. According to Chris, Nelson is laying low and relying on only one or two shifters to keep food and other supplies stocked in a few places. The drug stash in that shed was actually there for Nelson to pick up. He's desperate for cash, so he was hoping to find a way to make some. That's how Chris helps us. We've cut off one of Nelson's last supports. Chris also gave us location info on the places he thinks Nelson might be staying. Chris was stubborn at first, but once he came around, he's been helpful."

Vivi chewed on the inside of her cheek, her anxiety getting the best of her. She was still mulling over trying to talk to Chris. "What kind of deal would you make with Chris?"

Roger shrugged. "That's up to the prosecutor. In a case like this, they'd usually be looking at negotiating on the charges and reducing his time behind bars. We've got him solid on the possession with intent to distribute on a pretty large quantity, so his attorney is going to try to talk sense into him, which he already did." He paused for another swallow of coffee and grimaced. "Damn, coffee is crap today." He glanced back to Vivi. "You ready to go talk to him?"

Her stomach tightened with nervous dread mingled with anger. She didn't *want* to talk to Chris at all. If she hadn't gotten pregnant, he would simply be a one-off bad relationship. Instead he was linked to her forever because of Julianna. Julianna was the one and only reason Vivi was here to talk with Chris. She owed it to her. She met Roger's eyes. "Does he know I'm coming by?"

"Oh yeah. When we interviewed him earlier, I let him know you requested a meeting. Just so you know, he could refuse, but he didn't."

She stood from her chair. "Okay, let's go." She needed to get it over with. Since she'd last heard from Chris a few years ago, she'd replayed many hypothetical conversations with him in her head, most of which involved her telling him off and walking away with her head held high. He, of course, would be appropriately mortified and ashamed that he'd abandoned Julianna. But now, on the cusp of having her chance to talk to him, Vivi didn't know what she would say. If she tried to narrow it down, all she wanted was to know if he *ever* thought he wanted to be a part of Julianna's life. The problem was if the answer was yes, she had no idea what to do with that.

Roger stood from his desk and gulped down the last of his crap coffee before tossing the paper cup in the trashcan by the door. He gestured for her to follow him down the hall. They passed along a sterile gray hallway through a secure door into another hallway. Two more secure doors later and she stood beside Roger in front of a door that led into a room where Chris sat at a table. The room had a window, so her entire conversation with Chris would be observed. When she stood by the door without moving, Roger glanced her way.

"Having second thoughts?" he asked.

She'd known Roger for her entire life. They'd grown up in Painter together. She didn't recall how many years apart they'd been in school, but it was close enough they'd led parallel lives growing up. While he wasn't in her closest circle of friends, she trusted him completely. Ever since the rumors started swirling about the shifter smuggling network, she'd been mightily relieved Roger was on the police force. A few friendly shifters on the force were critical at any given point, but even more so lately. At the moment, she was relieved she knew Roger the way she did, otherwise she'd be embarrassed. She did and didn't want to talk with Chris. The indecision made her feel restless and out of sorts inside.

She turned to Roger. "Maybe, but I'm seeing this through. Are you waiting out here?" she asked, gesturing to the small room they stood inside. It was bare except for a few chairs and the window that looked into the room where Chris was waiting.

"Up to you. If you're uncomfortable with it, I'll leave. Everything in that room gets recorded though. He may offer up more information to you, so we don't want to miss it. Either I wait in here, or out in the hallway. Your call."

Vivi shrugged. "I don't have a damn thing to hide, so it doesn't matter to me." She took a fortifying breath. "Okay, let me in there."

Roger swiped his badge before the scanner on the door. At the sound of a soft click, he pushed it open and gestured her through. The door fell closed behind her. Chris glanced up from the table. He was handcuffed, which sent a jolt through her. No matter how she sliced it, it was strange to see Julianna's father sitting before her like this. Of all the things that had annoyed her about Chris after she came to understand him for who he was, she couldn't have prepared herself for this.

His blondish-brown hair was messier than usual. His brown eyes were weary and resigned. She considered that she'd once thought him quite handsome—a new shifter from out of town with a roguish smile and a wild edge. Looking at him now, she marveled that she'd ever been attracted to him. In hindsight, all she could do was wonder just what the hell she'd been thinking. Her stomach was still in knots, but she managed to walk to the small table and sit down across from him.

"Hi," she said simply, uncertain where to start.

Chris nodded, his eyes catching hers and bouncing away. "Hey. Uh, they mentioned you wanted to talk to me."

She sat there, her feelings of anger, disappointment and hurt dog-eared and worn. "Look, I'm not here because I give a damn about you. I'm only here because of Julianna. She's old enough to wonder who her father is and asks every so often. I guess I'd like to know if you ever plan to have anything to do with her."

Chris traced a finger along the steel edge of his handcuffs. He simply shook his head.

Anger flared hot inside of her. Her chest tightened and she had to force herself to take a gulp of air. She swallowed and looked over at him. "That's a no?"

Chris leaned back in his chair, his eyes cold and flat. "Obviously. Shifters don't like to be tied down. You knew that when you met me. Nothing's different now. Don't know why you ever thought it would be."

Chris's words hit her right in the gut. She'd known he'd glamorized that part of being a shifter—wild, free and not to be tied down. When he was nothing other than a shifter she found attractive and who called to her own wildness, it hadn't seemed to matter. Yet, then she had Julianna and everything tilted inside of her. She wanted Julianna to have a father who took care of her. She had struggled mightily to come to terms with how stupid she'd been. She hadn't wanted to cling to the thin thread of hope that Chris might actually be there for Julianna someday, but she had. The weight of telling Julianna this truth fell heavily on her shoulders.

"Go to hell," she said between her gritted teeth.

She pushed her chair back. It scraped against the concrete floor, the sound loud and harsh in the small room. She looked over at Chris once more. "At least have enough decency to give the police what they need to find Nelson."

At that, she turned and let herself out of the room. Roger was leaning against the far wall by the door. He pushed away and quickly opened the door leading into the hallway. Once they were in the hallway, Vivi picked up the pace. When she reached the next door, she turned impatiently toward Roger when he didn't immediately swipe his card to open the door. She gestured to the door. "Any day now."

Roger leaned his shoulder against the wall by the door. "Look, I'm sure you're pissed, but at least he was straight with you."

She shrugged and shifted on her feet. "Yeah. I didn't have high hopes, but it sucks for Julianna."

Roger eyed her for a long moment before he nodded and flashed his badge at the scanner by the lock. He held the door for her and escorted her down the next hallway and out to the entrance. She glanced over her shoulder when she stepped outside. "Thanks, Roger."

After a quick nod, he allowed the door to fall closed. She walked quickly to her car and climbed in. The anger she'd been holding in roared through her. She threw her purse on the passenger seat and pounded her fist against the steering wheel. She leaned back and sighed, the flash of anger fading as swiftly as it came. She pictured Julianna's wide brown eyes when she asked how come she didn't have a dad who lived with them. Her heart clenched with worry, hurt, and disappointment. For the thousandth time, she wished she'd had enough sense to see past the surface of Chris. The repeating loop of recrimination started there and ended with facing the odd fact that if it weren't for Chris, she wouldn't have Julianna, and Julianna was the best thing in her life by far.

She sighed and started her car. By the time she got home, an icy rain had started to fall. She ran inside and leaned against the door. Her emotions were a muddle. She couldn't help but wonder just why she'd allowed herself to start to be hopeful about Heath. *Foolish, foolish, foolish girl. How do you even know things could work out with him? You were just as stupidly hopeful about Chris and look at how that turned out.*

She pushed away from the door and shrugged out of her jacket, hanging it up on the coatrack by the door. After she toed her boots off, she heard the distinct sound of the school bus brakes outside. She stepped to the stove and turned on the burner under the teapot before walking to the door just as Julianna crested the top of the porch stairs. She raced inside and shook her head, her braids swinging back and forth, sending an arc of raindrops through the air.

"I got wet!"

Julianna's bright announcement broke through the fog of negative thoughts and brought a smile to Vivi's face, a smile that faded quickly when she considered the reality that her joyful daughter had a father who didn't give a damn. Even though she'd known this in some way for years, knowing it with certainty cut her to the core. She forced herself not to let her feelings show and focused on Julianna. Vivi angled her head to the side. "You don't say?"

Julianna giggled and shimmied out of her backpack while she kicked off her shoes. Vivi guessed Julianna must have waited outside in the rain for the bus because her jacket was nearly soaked through. The shoulders of her shirt were wet and her pants clung to her legs. When she saw a shudder run through Julianna, Vivi nudged her chin toward the bathroom. "How about you go hop in the bath? You're soaked and cold. That'll warm you up."

It was a reflection of how cold Julianna was that she nodded quickly and ran straight past Vivi to the bathroom. Vivi called out after her. "I'll make grilled cheese sandwiches for dinner."

After dinner in the living room and a half hour of television, Vivi tucked Julianna in and dropped a kiss on her forehead. "Night, sweetie."

"Night, Mom."

Vivi stood and walked quietly toward the door. Just before she reached it, Julianna's soft voice reached her. "When can we have Heath over for dinner again?"

Vivi's stomach fluttered and her chest felt tight. It was almost painful to have Julianna ask about Heath and a kick to her wishful thinking. After today, all she wanted was to shore herself up inside and make sure she protected Julianna. She couldn't trust herself to hope for much anymore. She paused at the door, her hand gripping the frame. "I'm not sure, sweetie. Next time I see him, I'll ask."

"Promise?"

"Of course. As soon as I see him, I'll find out."

She stepped through the door and quietly closed it. She walked quickly through the living room and sat down at the kitchen table. Resting her elbows on the table, she dropped her face into her hands. Her breath filtered through her fingers when she sighed. Already she'd let Heath in too far. She had no idea how to navigate this. Facing the brutal truth of finding a way to be honest with Julianna about Chris, she couldn't think about trying to hope for the best with Heath. Not now. She dropped her hands from her face and sat up when her phone vibrated on the table. She reached a hand out and spun the phone across the table. Heath's name flashed on the screen, along with another text. He'd texted a few times this afternoon. She'd initially tried to ignore them because she just wasn't up for dealing with him on top of facing Chris. She'd eventually chosen to reply in the hopes he would leave her alone at least for the night. She wasn't proud of it, but she'd told him she had a migraine.

She tapped the screen open and read his latest text. *Hope you get some rest and feel better tonight. Will call tomorrow.*

Her fingertips itched to type a reply, but she forced herself to set the phone down. The part of her heart that longed for Heath to be the person she turned to for support couldn't be running the show. She had to stay strong and stand on her own two feet, like she'd been doing for years. Restless, she stood and headed for the shower, as if she could wash away her muddled feelings. Afterwards, she tumbled into a fitful night of sleep. When she woke the following morning, she went through the motions of helping Julianna get ready for school and watched her run through the rain to climb on the bus.

When her phone vibrated and she saw another text from Heath, she made an abrupt decision. She couldn't trust herself to know if she was ready for a relationship, and she certainly couldn't trust herself to know if it made a lick of sense to let herself fall so deeply in with anyone. She didn't know how to navigate any of this, especially when it came to Julianna. She snagged her phone and called Heath.

As soon as he picked up, she started talking. "I can't do this. I know you probably want to talk about it, but there's no point. Not right now. I have to focus on Julianna, and I just don't think now is the time to try to any kind of relationship." She paused to gulp in air.

Heath started to say something, but she cut him off. She couldn't tolerate how she felt—a mix of anger, fear, and a desperate need to *not* need anyone, especially when her heart was so fragile. "I have to go. I'm sorry." She ended the call and tossed her phone across the room. It hit the wall and thudded against the floor. She didn't even bother to pick it up. She sat down at the kitchen table, the chair almost toppling over when she landed on the edge.

Chapter 14

Heath immediately tried to call Vivi back when the line went silent. The phone rang and rang. He grabbed his coat and yanked it on as he ran outside into the rain to climb in his truck. He started to race over to her house, but came to an abrupt stop when he was about to turn onto Main Street. Even though he was frantic to see her and talk to her, he knew her well enough to know it probably wasn't going to help if he tried to push right now. With his stomach coiled with dread and frustration coursing through him, he turned in the opposite direction and headed down to the police station. He didn't know what had transpired yesterday, but he knew she'd gone to talk with Chris at the jail. Maybe Roger could shed some light on what was going on.

A few minutes later, he walked into the police station. He gave his jacket a shake to knock the rain free. Roger must have seen him pull up in the parking lot because he met him inside the reception area.

"Come on back," Roger said, holding the door for Heath to follow him into the hallway that led to the offices.

"Coffee?" Roger asked as he paused to pour himself a cup from the coffee pot stationed on a table by his office door.

"Nah. I'm good."

"Suit yourself." Roger led the way into his office and closed the door behind Heath. He snagged a chair by the table and gestured for Heath to sit across from him. "I can guess why you're here."

"Why's that?" Heath countered.

"Vivi didn't look too happy when she left after her meeting with Chris. Have you seen her?"

Heath leaned back with a sigh and shook his head. "Nope. But she called me and basically told me to stay away. I was wondering what the hell happened when she talked to Chris yesterday."

"Seems like she wanted to know if he ever planned to act like a father. He made it clear that would never happen. She didn't seem upset for herself, but for Julianna."

Heath absorbed that and shrugged a shoulder. "We talked about it the night before last. She said she just wanted a chance to know his plans. I guess I figured she'd adjusted to the fact he hasn't been around." He swallowed against the tightness in his chest and throat. He didn't like feeling torn asunder by his feelings for her. He sure as hell didn't want to look as messy as he felt inside. Roger was a friend, but Heath wasn't exactly up for a relationship chat with him. Or with anyone, for that matter. He mentally shook himself. "How'd your interview go with Chris?"

"After he stewed and stalled, his court appointed attorney met with him. They know we've got Chris on some solid possession charges, so they must've leaned on him to be sensible. He opened up after that. It's nothing we didn't suspect, but he confirmed a lot of details. He's been helping Nelson with the pick ups and drop offs for the last year or so. Not that it matters a whole hell of a lot, but anything we get is leverage."

"Why was he holding onto that stash in the shed? I mean, it's been months since Nelson disappeared. Far as we knew, the smuggling mostly dried up because Nelson wasn't there to coordinate."

Roger nodded. "Exactly. According to Chris, what few stashes Nelson had left were unknown to anyone else in the network. Chris had moved that quantity from one place to another ever since we started searching properties and tearing down any storage locations. He figured we'd already searched that property, so it'd be a safer spot. Nelson planned to smuggle it himself for some cash. Chris doesn't seem to know if anyone else is left helping Nelson like he was. He also doesn't know where Nelson is, although he does know a few of the places he was hiding out. I was hoping to get with you and Daniel and head out in the next few days. I figure once Nelson realizes Chris has been brought in, he'll fan out again. Chris gave us three locations, two in Wyoming and one a few hours north in Colorado. We've searched the two in Wyoming because they're properties Daniel inherited. The one in Colorado is new to us. I checked it on a map and it's on Federal land. I'll send two teams to the other locations and was hoping you and Daniel would come with me to the one closer by."

"I'll be there whenever you want. Pretty sure Daniel will be too. Any idea when?"

"I'm aiming for the end of the week if that works for you guys. Much as I'd like to head out right away, Nelson will be expecting us. I'd like to wait a few days, so he might let down his guard."

Heath stood from the table. "Just call me. I'll let Daniel know when I see him."

When Heath reached the door, Roger spoke.

"Heath."

"Yeah?"

"Give Vivi a little time. She'll come around."

Heath appreciated Roger's sentiment, but he was feeling impatient and frustrated—not exactly helpful at the moment. "Hope so. Catch you later." Heath lifted his hand in a wave and left.

Heath headed over to Mile High Grounds. He needed to see if Sophia had any clue what was going on with Vivi. The coffee shop was a warm haven on the cold, rainy day. Usually, he'd breathe a sigh of relief and relax once he stepped inside, but today he was too twisted up inside over Vivi. He strode to the counter, dragging his forearm across his face to wipe the rain away.

Sophia glanced up. She opened her mouth and closed it, her eyes narrowing. "What's wrong?"

"Can we start with some coffee?" Heath countered, a thread of irritation rising to have Sophia pick up on the fact he was off balance.

"Sure. What's your preference today?"

"Something strong."

Sophia glanced to Tommy at the espresso machine behind her. "Work your magic," she called to him.

"Got it." Tommy nodded in Heath's direction. "I'll add an extra shot to an Americano. How's that sound?"

"Sounds good," Heath replied. He leaned against the wall by the counter, reflexively looking toward the door when the bell chimed.

A couple walked in and approached the counter. Sophia took their order and put their selected pastries on two small plates. While she was helping them, Tommy quickly came from behind the espresso machine and slid Heath's coffee across the counter. "Enjoy," he said before turning back to get started in the next order.

Heath took a swallow and sighed, the flavor strong and rich. "Perfect!" he called out to Tommy who threw a grin his way.

After the couple stepped aside and sat down at a table, Sophia turned back to Heath. "Okay, something's wrong. What's up?"

"I was hoping you'd know."

"Clearly I don't."

"Vivi met with Chris yesterday. She blew me off last night and said she didn't feel good. This morning, she…well, I guess she kinda dumped me."

Sophia's eyes widened. "What? What did she say?"

Heath took a gulp of coffee, as if it could somehow fortify him. Inside, his gut was churning and his heart ached. He just wanted a chance to talk to Vivi, but she wasn't giving him one, so he'd try to intuit what he could from Sophia. She was Vivi's closest friend. If anyone could guess at what was going through Vivi's mind, it would be Sophia.

"She said she didn't think now was the time to try a relationship and she needed to focus on Julianna. She didn't give me a chance to talk about anything. That's it. I was hoping you'd have some idea what happened."

Sophia was quiet for several beats. Just when Heath was about to ask her what she thought again, Tommy called her name. She swung around and quickly grabbed the two coffee drinks Tommy passed to her. Without pause, she slipped from behind the counter and delivered the coffees to the couple at their table. When she returned to her station by the register, she looked to Heath, her eyes concerned. "I don't know what happened since she talked to Chris, but I can guess at what's going on. This whole thing with you, well, it took her off guard. I don't doubt for a second that she wants you. But you have to understand what it was like for her the first couple of years after she had Julianna. She was barely getting by. Her parents helped, but Vivi wanted to be able do things on her own. My guess is talking to Chris just brought up all her doubts about whether things can work out. Because of how he's been, well, just gone from Julianna's life, Vivi's really protective of her. I can't tell you what to do right now, but maybe give her a little space. It might help if you find a way to let her know you'll be there no matter what."

Heath gulped his coffee. "So I'm supposed to give her space *and* I should tell her I'll be there for her no matter what? How the hell am I supposed to do both things at once?"

Sophia's shoulders dropped with her sigh. "I don't know." She smiled ruefully. "I guess you can't."

"Don't see how I can."

***

A few days later, Heath stared into the edge of the forest. "How far away are we?" he asked, turning to Roger who stood to one side of him with Daniel standing on the other side.

Roger shrugged. "All I've got is a good guess based on what Chris told us. From here, the aerial maps show the old hunting cabin to be about two miles from here. Not far really."

Heath spun in a slow circle. They were parked in a small parking area along the outskirts of the forest. The road leading here wound through the mountains. The direction they were headed started level and angled upward steeply into the mountains.

"I'd say we get going while we have plenty of daylight," Daniel commented.

"Agreed," Heath added.

"Yup. Let's do this," Roger said.

They'd talked at length on the drive up, so there was no further need for planning. With three of them, they would mostly stick together, but if they picked up Nelson's scent, they'd agreed Roger would separate out and loop around from another angle. Without another word, they stepped into the trees and shifted. In seconds, they were jogging in unison through the forest, slowly winding their way deeper into the mountains.

Heath stretched into his lion, letting the power course through him in surges. He'd spent three days leaving Vivi alone, though it had taken every ounce of discipline he had. He was still spinning circles in his head and heart over how to break through this impasse with her. He didn't doubt they would eventually get past this, but it was nearly killing him to wait. Yet, he knew he had to. Of the many qualities he loved about Vivi, her strength and independence were high on the list. He knew she had to be ready on her terms. He was still pondering Sophia's conflicting advice to also find a way to let Vivi know he'd be there no matter what.

He'd hoped a few hours in lion form would help him think more clearly. He'd conveniently forgotten how his feelings intensified when his cat was free. The mere thought of Vivi tightened his heart and sent a wild combination of longing and frustration through him. He shook himself and forced his attention to where they were. The air was just above freezing. Autumn was winding down with winter closing in behind it. Roger and Daniel ran alongside him as they made their way through the trees.

The ground became rockier as they ascended into the mountains. As Roger indicated, they didn't have far to go before a small cabin was visible. It was an old hunting cabin that had been transformed into a camping hut for hikers in the area. They didn't expect to find Nelson here, but they hoped to catch his scent and follow it. They fanned out and circled the cabin in the trees. No sign of Nelson, however they caught his scent as they'd hoped.

They moved quietly and purposefully, honed in on the faint traces Nelson left behind. His trail eventually led through a small valley and ascended again onto a ridge. Simply by chance, Heath ended up in the lead. He picked his way carefully along a ledge that followed the curve of the mountainside. There was a sudden flash of motion. Heath saw a blur of tawny gold when Nelson leapt out from just ahead on the trail. With a vicious swipe, he knocked Heath off balance. Heath tumbled off the ledge, landing hard on the rocky ground below. Heath scrambled up with a roar. Daniel and Roger were already in the thick of a fight with Nelson by the time Heath regained his footing. When Daniel glanced down from the ledge and saw Heath was standing, he gave Nelson a strategic shove with his shoulder, sending Nelson tumbling to the ground beside Heath. Heath spun and tackled Nelson.

Daniel and Roger both leapt down from the ledge. The next few moments passed rapidly. Even though there were three of them, Nelson fought back viciously and didn't give up. Driven by his lingering anger over the scourge Nelson brought into Painter and the risk he brought upon shifters, Heath didn't back down and took some of Nelson's hardest blows. Nelson fought with a tinge of angry desperation, although his anger and emotional turmoil couldn't match Heath's. Between his own brush with the smuggling network and the recent events with Vivi, his feelings were knotted tight. He savored the release that came from the brutal fight and was oblivious to any pain. By the time they managed to subdue him, Heath was battered and scratched and Nelson was barely conscious.

They had to carry him out of the mountains. It was slow going and darkness was falling when they reached Roger's car. Roger bundled Nelson into the back of the car. He glanced between Heath and Daniel, his eyes swinging back to Heath. "Think we need to get you to the hospital. I'm not so sure we should wait to drive all the way back to Painter."

Heath was still coasting on adrenaline and didn't feel much of anything other than weary. "Nah. I'm fine. Let's go."

Roger looked to Daniel as if asking for back up. Daniel's eyes quickly scanned over Heath. "Roger has a point. Let's…"

Heath shook his head sharply. He figured if he needed immediate medical attention, he wouldn't be able to stand. "Forget it. Unless I pass out, drive until we get to Painter."

"I'll ride in the back," Daniel offered.

Since riding in the back meant being closer to Nelson, Heath shrugged. When he reached for the door handle to climb into the car, he started to become aware of his condition. Sharp pain shot from his shoulder down through his arm. He fumbled to open the door and collapsed in the car seat. The drive back to Painter was long and more painful than Heath had considered. Stubbornness kept him from saying a word. By the time Roger turned onto Main Street in Painter, Heath was beyond exhausted and gritting his teeth from the pain. He'd narrowed the worst injuries down to his shoulder and the side of his neck where Nelson must have scratched him deeply. It hurt to breathe, so he figured he also might have broken a few ribs.

Roger pulled up in front of the hospital and glanced over his shoulder. He said something to Daniel, but everything sounded muted to Heath. He felt as if he was floating underwater in a blur of pain and exhaustion. A few minutes later, Daniel was standing beside him where he sat on an examining table. The last thing Heath remembered was how much he wanted to talk to Vivi.

Chapter 15

The mug Vivi held slipped from her hands and fell, breaking into shards with coffee splattering around it on the kitchen floor. Inside she felt about the same way. She turned and leaned her hip against the counter, fumbling to keep the phone held to her ear.

"What do you mean?" she asked Sophia.

"Heath's in the hospital. I'm on my way right now," Sophia replied, her voice strained.

"What happened?" Vivi asked, a sense of panic rising inside.

"Like I told you the other night, he and Daniel were planning to go with Roger to look for Nelson. They found him and brought him in, but I guess Heath took the brunt of punishment in the fight with Nelson. Daniel just called me to tell me he's at the hospital with Heath."

Vivi heard a beep on the line and then another. "Do you know if he's okay?" Vivi asked, fear spiraling wildly inside and her heart lodged in her throat.

The connection crackled in her ear, so Sophia's reply was broken up.

"Say that again. I can't hear…"

Sophia cut in. "Look, I have to go. My mom's calling on the other line. Meet me at the hospital."

The line went dead in Vivi's ear and panic nearly choked her. She struggled to take a full breath and slowly set the phone down. A strange mix of numbness combined with a wild desperation rendered her motionless as she tried to get her body under control. Her heart pounded and she couldn't seem to get enough air in her lungs. She'd spent the last few days clinging to the idea that she needed time to think clearly and to proceed carefully with Heath. Every time she thought about how damn stupid she'd been with Chris and what it meant for Julianna, the internal recriminations just wouldn't quit. Even though she knew Heath was nothing like Chris, it didn't mean she could trust herself to know she wasn't jumping too fast and too deep into something.

Now, Heath was injured badly enough to be in the hospital. All she could think about was how fast she could get to him and if she'd already blown it with him. She broke out of the frozen feeling inside and went into action. She started to run out of the kitchen only to slip on the coffee-wet floor and fall. She caught most of her weight on her palm and cried out when one of the broken pieces of the mug dug into her skin. She curled her knees under her and lifted her hand. She carefully knocked away the offending pottery shard and glanced around at the mess surrounding her. She'd sustained a deep puncture just below her thumb. She barely even noticed the pain with her entire focus on getting to Heath as quickly as she could. She climbed to her feet and walked to the bathroom. After quickly cleaning and bandaging her hand, she swept up the broken mug and wiped up the coffee before she left. On her way out, she called her mother and asked if Julianna could stay for the night. Julianna had already spent the afternoon there because a friend from school who lived nearby had invited her over for a homework club.

"Thanks Mom. I'll call you as soon as I have an update, okay?"

"Of course. It's never a problem to have Julianna here. Please let Heath know I'm thinking of him, okay?"

Vivi's pulse was racing along at a rapid, unsettled pace. Her mother's words sent it into overdrive. "Right. I just hope…oh hell, I just hope he's okay."

"Vivi?" her mother asked after Vivi was silent for longer than usual.

"Huh?"

"Try to breathe, and listen to what your heart's telling you."

Her mother's comment snapped her out of her fuzzy thoughts. "What?"

"Just what I said. Call me when you have some news."

At that, her mother hung up. Vivi stared ahead as she kept driving. Her house wasn't too far from the hospital, but it felt like forever right now. The streetlights glittered in the darkness. The tiniest bit of tension eased when she saw the bright lights from the hospital parking lot. She parked rapidly and jogged to the entrance. Every step of the way, all she could think about was making sure Heath was okay. She ran through the doors and to the main desk in the emergency room area.

She skidded to a stop by the desk. "I need to see Heath Ashworth," she said abruptly.

The nurse glanced up. "Are you family?"

"Well, no, but I might as well be."

The nurse shook her head. "I'm sorry, but we can't give any information out unless you're family."

The woman looked back at her computer and kept on typing. Anger rose swiftly inside Vivi. "What the hell is wrong with you? People don't just show up at hospitals to see someone unless they give a damn. Please tell me…" Her voice raised an octave with every word, but she was conveniently interrupted when she felt a hand curl around her elbow.

She turned to find Sophia at her side. "Come on. We're all waiting down the hall." Sophia's eyes were warm and worried.

Vivi threw a final glare at the nurse behind the desk, although she'd turned around and didn't even see it. She hurried along at Sophia's side. "What's going on? Do we know if he's okay?"

Sophia nodded, her mouth pinched and her face tense. "He's in surgery. He insisted he was okay when they left, but he should've gone straight to the closest hospital. Instead, Roger and Daniel didn't push it and he lost a lot of blood on the way here. I guess he has a nasty tear on one side of his neck and shoulder. The doctor is operating right now to close it up. Apparently, Nelson came within centimeters of his carotid artery. Heath is damn lucky he's alive."

Vivi absorbed Sophia's words and swallowed against the cold fear rolling through her. Her throat was tight and her heart ached. Sophia turned into a waiting area where Daniel sat, along with Heath and Sophia's parents, Leo and Lila Ashworth. Lila stood when they entered the room and immediately came to Vivi's side, pulling her into a warm hug. When she stepped back, she slid her hands down Vivi's arms. "I'm glad you're here. Heath would want you to be here," Lila said, her dark brown eyes warm and assessing. Her almost black hair was streaked with silver and pulled back into a loose ponytail.

Lila might as well have been a second mother to Vivi. The same could be said for Vivi's mother to Sophia. They'd spent so much of their childhoods at each other's houses that it was impossible not to feel that way. Vivi wondered what Lila knew of her and Heath. When she met her eyes, she knew Lila was at least aware something was going on between them. Vivi saw the kind understanding and concern reflected in her gaze and almost burst into tears. She took a deep breath and tried to calm the worry and fear coiling tightly inside.

"Do we know how long it will be before we hear from the doctor again?" she asked.

Lila shook her head. "All we know is they took him into surgery. The nurse who checked in last said it would be at least another hour before he's moved into recovery."

An hour seemed too long and terrifying. That sense of panic clogged her throat again, making it hard to breathe.

Lila slid her hands down to squeeze Vivi's, prompting Vivi to flinch from the cut on her palm. Lila lifted her hand and turned it over. "What happened to you? Are you okay?"

Vivi nodded quickly. "Just a little cut. No big deal." As the words left her mouth, all she could think was it was nothing compared to what Heath was going through.

When Lila dropped her hands and moved to sit again, Vivi followed suit and turned to Daniel. "What happened?"

Daniel quickly offered a summary of events. "Honestly, Heath took a pretty big fall when Nelson knocked him off the ledge. You have to understand, it was a muddle for a few minutes. Heath just wouldn't back down and neither would Nelson. When we tried to persuade Heath to go to the hospital up there, he refused. If I'd known how deep Nelson had gotten him, I'd have insisted."

Daniel clearly felt responsible and shook his head, a look of worry and frustration in his eyes.

Sophia slipped her hand into his where it rested on his thigh. "It's okay. Heath's going to be okay. We just have to wait to find out how he's doing after surgery."

Vivi leaned her head against the wall behind her and tried to corral her feelings. She'd been such an idiot. She loved Heath. She'd loved him for years. She'd let her own fear get in the way. Now, she was afraid he might not make it through this, and she might not have a chance to tell him how she felt. After everything he'd been through over the last year, she couldn't stop worrying that it was worse than they knew. The next hour crawled by. The television in the waiting room rumbled in the background. She mostly tuned it out until her ears perked up when Nelson's name was announced. She wasn't alone with everyone in the waiting room turning to the television. The stately local news anchor continued what he was saying.

"We received a report from the police in Painter, Colorado this evening that they believe Nelson Weaver was the original mastermind and organizer for the drug smuggling network. The network sprung up in Painter and then spread throughout Colorado and into other states over the last few years. As you've heard from previous reports, law enforcement in multiple states have been gradually taking the network down, but the authorities here reported slow progress except for arrests of low level dealers. Last summer, they had a big break when they identified Mr. Weaver as the leader of the drug ring, but he was believed to be in hiding for months. Law enforcement chose not to release his name to the public in order to protect their investigation. Reports indicate Mr. Weaver was arrested this afternoon on Federal lands several hours north of Painter. This won't mean the end of drugs or of smuggling, but the authorities do believe Mr. Weaver's arrest was crucial and will eliminate a significant source of drugs coming into the area."

Vivi sighed and glanced around the room. She should feel elated, but she couldn't feel anything other than worry and fear right now. If Heath wasn't okay, Nelson's arrest would mean they paid much too high of a price to bring him down. She idly traced the edge of the bandage on her palm and waited. She'd lost track of how long they'd been waiting when a nurse stepped into the room. Vivi leapt out of her chair, while the rest of the family circled the nurse.

The nurse, a slender woman with warm blue eyes and short brown hair, smiled at them. "Well, I can see Mr. Ashworth has plenty of family concerned about him. You'll be glad to know the surgery went well. He's in the recovery room now and can have visitors shortly."

The nurse was bombarded with questions from the others, while Vivi leaned against the wall and put her hands over her face. She didn't need to know anything other than that Heath was safe and okay. Immense relief swept through her. She felt a hand curl over her shoulder and glanced up to find Lila beside her.

"Are you okay, dear?" Lila asked softly.

Vivi nodded and swallowed through the tightness in her throat. "Uh huh. I'm just…" She paused and took a shaky breath. When she met Lila's eyes again, the tears rolled down her cheeks. Vivi swiped at them. "You must think I'm an idiot. Here you are doing just fine and Heath's your son. I'm, oh, I don't know…"

When her words trailed off, Lila slipped her arm across Vivi's shoulders and tugged her into another hug. When she released her, Lila leaned against the wall beside Vivi. "Heath loves you. You know that, right?"

Vivi bit her lip and rolled her head to the side to look at Lila. "I think so. I haven't handled things all that well."

Lila smiled softly. "You've handled things just fine. I talked to Heath the other day and told him to give you some time. Julianna *should* be your priority. I never needed to sort through something like that, but every mother knows you don't just bring a new man into your child's life without finding a way to do it very carefully. I believe you probably love Heath too, but that still doesn't mean you should rush things."

Somehow Lila's way of framing the issue, without judgment and as if it made perfect sense, eased the knot of uncertainty and tension Vivi had been holding inside for weeks. Vivi took in a gulp of air and closed her eyes. When she opened them, she glanced to Lila. "I do love him. I just hope he understands I didn't mean to hurt him."

Lila reached over and squeezed Vivi's good hand. "He already understands. I'm not going to pretend he's enjoyed the last few days, but he understands. If not, just give me a call and I'll knock the sense back into him."

Vivi laughed softly, her tears still hot in her eyes. "I'll do that."

A few minutes later, the doctor came to offer more of an update on Heath's surgery and what to expect next. They were then allowed into the recovery room to visit him, only two at a time. Even though Vivi was desperate to see Heath, she felt his parents and Sophia needed to see him first, so she hung back and waited while they went in in pairs. When she was finally in the room beside him, the tears welled again. His eyes were closed when she approached the hospital bed. The recovery room didn't offer much privacy. His bed was surrounded with a curtain, and she could hear the soft mumble of other voices nearby.

She quietly sat down in the chair situated beside the bed. His breathing was slow and even. She didn't want to disturb him, so she carefully slipped her hand onto the bed where his rested and eased hers over it. His breathing didn't change, so she stayed like that, softly stroking her thumb over the back of his palm. After a few minutes, he rolled his head to the side and opened his eyes. For a second, they were unfocused. He blinked and then his dark green gaze held hers. He started to sit up, but fell back against the bed.

"Don't move!" she whispered fiercely, fighting against the tears welling inside.

"I'm fine," he said, his voice hoarse.

"You are *not* fine. You just had surgery," she said, trying to inject some sternness in her tone.

He somehow managed a small shrug with one shoulder, although he grimaced when he did. He turned his hand over and laced his fingers into hers. "I didn't think I was in bad shape. Last thing I remember is Daniel telling me I collapsed when we got here."

Her heart felt sliced open. She tried and failed to keep the tears from spilling down her cheeks. His hand gripped hers tightly. "Please don't cry, Vivi. It's okay. I'm okay."

She nodded and dragged her forearm across her face, smearing her tears on her sleeve. "I know, I know. But you got hurt, and I got scared." She paused and gulped in air. "Maybe now's not the best time to talk, but I'm sorry. I'm so sorry I got all freaked out. Its just...it's just you mean so much to me."

Heath again tried to sit up and fell back.

"Stop it. You're going to hurt yourself."

His mouth hooked in a half-smile. "Hard to get in worse shape than I was before the surgery." His smile faded. "I love you, you know."

Her tears kept rolling down her cheeks. She squeezed his hand tightly and nodded. "I love you. I do, I really do. I just…ugh." She paused for another breath of air. "I talked to Chris and it made me question everything. Not about you, but about me. I mean, he's, well, he's a complete loser and I was dumb enough to fall for him. Julianna has a fool for a father and I can't do anything to change that. I want to make sure I do what's right for her. Somehow I got that all mixed up into thinking I needed to keep you out of our lives." She shook her head sharply. "But I love you and that isn't going to change, so I figure it's better if I find a way to deal with that instead of running away from it."

Heath's eyes locked onto hers, his expression somber and soft at once. She felt held by his gaze alone. She could feel the beat of his pulse against her wrist. "My mom told me I needed to be patient, but I won't pretend the last few days didn't suck." He cleared his throat. "I can't do anything about Chris and how he's treated Julianna, but I promise you I already love her as if she was mine. I don't want to replace her father in her mind, but as far as I'm concerned, she's my daughter. I know she comes first for you, and she's first for me too. Okay?"

She nodded, unable to speak a word with the flood of emotions coursing through her. At that moment, the distinct sound of the curtain sliding on its track came. Vivi glanced over her shoulder to see the nurse peeking around the edge of the curtain. "Sorry to interrupt, but I need to check on a few things. Will that be okay?"

Vivi started to stand, but the nurse shook her head. It was the same nurse who'd come to let them know Heath's surgery went well. Her blue eyes coasted over Heath. "You're looking quite well for what you've been through today, Mr. Ashworth," the nurse offered with a soft

J.H. Croix

smile.

Heath held tight to Vivi's hand and grinned. "I've been worse. What do you need to check on?"

The nurse stepped to the far side of the bed and scanned the monitor positioned on that side. "Just making sure your vitals are still stable, which they are." She reached up and checked the fluid in the IV bag hanging from its stand. "How's your pain?" she asked as she turned to face the bed.

Heath shrugged. "I can deal with it. If you don't mind, I'd prefer you keep any doses of pain medication light."

The nurse arched a brow in question.

"I was in a bad car accident over a year ago and had a rough time coming off the painkillers. I'd rather live with a little extra pain than go through that again," Heath explained matter-of-factly.

The nurse nodded firmly. "Understood. I'll let the doctor know." She turned to leave, but Heath spoke again.

"Not to sound stupid, but do you mind telling me what the surgery was for? I don't remember a damn thing after I got here except waking up briefly to hear my buddy tell me I passed out."

The nurse grinned. "You sure did. Fell in a heap at his feet, as a matter of fact." She sobered. "You sustained a nasty puncture wound on your neck and a deep scratch that ran down your neck and shoulder. Your friend said you fell while you guys were out hiking and caught your shoulder on a branch. That must've been one sharp branch because it did a bit of damage. The doctor took care of some other scratches and nicks, so you've got stitches in a few places. The other areas would probably heal up on their own, but since he was operating, we wanted to minimize chances of infection. You'll need to stay for a few hours, but you can probably go home later tonight. No need for you to stay overnight." At that, she glanced between them. "I'll let you two have a few more minutes to yourselves. Visitors are only allowed in recovery for fifteen minutes at a time." At that, the nurse slipped through the curtain. It fell behind her with a soft whoosh.

Heath had never released Vivi's hand, his grip surprisingly strong given his physical state. His eyes scanned Vivi's face, warmth, affinity, love and a hint of fire held there.

Epilogue

Heath leaned over the kitchen table and stared at Julianna's math worksheet. "Word problems," he said, prompting a giggle from Julianna who sat beside him.

He glanced to her. Her dark hair was braided into two long braids, its usual style. She was such an active girl that if her hair was left loose, it became a tangled mess quickly. One foot swung back and forth as she doodled in the margin of her worksheet. "How about I help you with the measurement stuff? That's where I'm the expert. Word problems, not so much."

Julianna turned to him and wrinkled her nose, her brown eyes glinted with mirth. "I already did these. It's your job to check them," she said, a giggle escaping at the end.

"Oh, right. Okay, hand it over."

"You didn't even read far enough to see I already did them," Julianna said with mock sternness as she slid the paper in front of him.

"I'm reading them now," he countered, eliciting another giggle from her.

A few minutes later, he handed the worksheet back to her and proclaimed her homework done for the night. Julianna tucked the worksheet in her folder and slipped from her chair to return the folder to her backpack. Jax tackled her feet, a blur of black and white as he scampered away and dashed into the living room. Julianna chased after him, leaving Heath alone at the kitchen table.

He glanced over at Vivi who slid a tray of Julianna's beloved crunchy mac and cheese into the oven and closed it. She tossed the oven mitt on the counter and snagged a bottle of wine sitting on the counter, along with two glasses from the cabinet. She sat across from him and filled the glasses, holding hers up for a toast. "To homework!"

The clink of their glasses was muted amidst the squeals of Julianna in the living room as she played with Jax. Heath looked over at Vivi, his heart clenching. His mind spun back to the night, over a year ago, when she insisted he come home with her after his altercation with Nelson and subsequent visit to the emergency room. In the time since, their lives had become stitched tightly together. He couldn't conceive of life without her and Julianna.

She set her wineglass on the table and he leaned across, nudging her chin up with his knuckles and catching her lips in a quick kiss. It didn't matter the time or place, all he had to do was be near her and his body hummed. He leaned back in his chair and took a gulp of his wine. With Julianna nearby, he needed to keep his body on leash. Vivi's cheeks were flushed. She set her wineglass down and rested her elbows on the table.

"So, did you happen to hear from Roger today?"

He nodded. "Oh yeah. He called me as soon as the trial was over. The prosecution got what they wanted for Nelson—minimum of twenty years behind bars. It's a damn relief to have that over."

In the intervening time since Nelson had been caught, they'd both been tied up in some way or another with the legal proceedings. The shifter smuggling network had finally been extinguished in Painter. Heath was cynical enough to know something like it would probably resurface somehow someday, but what Nelson created had staggered and fallen once the police figured out how he was using the many old logging properties for storage and transfers.

Vivi took a sip of wine and trailed her fingers along the stem of her glass. "I'll say. Took too damn long, but he'll be locked up for a good long time." She lifted her eyes and scanned his face. "I'm so glad you're okay." Her words came out raspy.

He reached for her hand and gave it a squeeze. "Of course I am. Trust me, that last fight wasn't so bad. It was the year before that nearly killed me," he said, referencing his car accident and tumble into painkiller addiction. He didn't talk about it much, but it had been a frightening time for him. He'd felt lost—as a man and as a lion. He recalled thinking he could never be the man and shifter Vivi deserved. He hadn't thought of it at the time, but being part of finally bringing Nelson in had helped him find closure around the path he'd stumbled upon after his car accident. He felt a sense of satisfaction in knowing he'd helped end the scourge of what Nelson created.

Vivi's voice brought Heath back to the moment. "Maybe you thought it was not much, but it scared me to death." Her eyes glistened, and she bit her lip. "I suppose the good thing is it made me get over myself."

At that moment, Julianna came skidding into the kitchen, dragging a tattered piece of yarn behind her on the floor. Jax was pouncing and hissing at the innocent yarn. Heath turned to look at Julianna, and his chest almost ached. Somehow he'd not only made it back to the man and shifter he once was, but he'd flat lucked out and stumbled into the love of his life with the blessing of her strong-willed joyous daughter along with her.

A while later, crunchy mac and cheese long gone, Heath lay in bed and listened to the sound of Vivi's breathing. Her head was resting on his shoulder and her leg thrown across both of his. Her lush curves were soft and warm against his side. He stroked a palm down her back and fell asleep to the rhythm of her breath.

***

"Where are we going and why do I have to wear this?" Vivi asked, as she felt Heath tighten the cotton bandana around her head.

He'd shown up at the door, waving the bandana and insisting she come with him on a drive, although he adamantly refused to tell her where they were going. He finished knotting the bandana. "You'll just have to wait and see." At that, he closed the truck door.

Seconds later, she heard him get in on the driver's side. She felt him turn onto Main Street, but after that she lost track of where he could be going. He drove roughly ten minutes before she felt another turn and the sound of gravel crunching under the tires. Moments later, he was opening the passenger door and helping her out. She tried to shake him off and reached to untie the bandana, but he caught her hands in his and firmly pulled her along with him.

"Just let me surprise you, okay?" he asked, a low laugh escaping after his question.

"Fine," she huffed as she walked alongside him.

They came to a stop. Without sight, her other senses were heightened. She heard the distant call of a crow and the sound of water running over rocks nearby. The air was woodsy. She surmised they were on the edge of the forest.

After a moment of quiet, Heath moved to stand behind her and untied the bandana. When he slipped it away and she opened her eyes, a gorgeous cedar home stood before her, tucked into the edge of a slope. The slope leveled out behind the house into a small field through which a wide stream ran. Her eyes followed the stream up where it disappeared into the trees marching up the mountains in back of the home. The home was clearly new and the ground around it was still freshly turned. Puzzled, she turned to Heath who'd come to stand at her side.

"Is this one of your latest projects? It's beautiful. I'm sure the owners are happy with what you've done."

His green gaze caught hers, a slow smile spreading across his face. "You think it's beautiful?"

"Of course! Every house you design is beautiful. Mind telling me why you brought me out here to see it? I don't mind, but…"

"It's for us."

Her heart flew skyward inside and tears instantly pressed at the back of her eyes. She gasped and stared at him for a long moment before swinging to look at the house again. "For us? Really?"

He stepped in front of her and reached for her hands, which were chilly in the late autumn air. The warmth of his touch radiated through her. "Really. I started planning it last winter and worked on it all summer. It's ready to go. I, uh…" he paused and cleared his throat "wanted to make sure you knew without a doubt that I wanted our lives to be together." She felt him trace the edge of the engagement ring he'd given her a few weeks prior. She'd thought he couldn't do more to knot her heart with his, but he'd gone and done it. She thought back to the number of times she'd commented on her tiny house over the last few months and marveled at how well he'd kept this secret.

She tipped her face up and freed her hands, bringing them up to cup his cheeks, the stubble rough under her touch. "You have no idea how much I love this. I can't believe you went to all this work. Just for us…"

Heath dipped his head and caught her lips in a fierce kiss. He pulled back only a fraction. She could feel his lips move against hers when he spoke. "The work was nothing. I'm just glad you love it. Come on, let's go inside."

He turned and tugged for her to follow. The interior was as beautiful as the outside. The main living area was bright and filled with light. The living room stretched into a kitchen. The floors were polished hardwood with cedar ceilings above. The kitchen was modern and sleek, but had a warm feeling with soft green polished granite counters and birch cabinets. The living room faced the mountains with a massive stone fireplace occupying one wall. The home managed to feel spacious and cozy at once. Given that it was currently empty of furniture, Vivi marveled at how it felt inside. There were four bedrooms, including a large master suite with its own bathroom. Vivi considered how mornings went these days—a constant juggle of who needed the bathroom when. Heath had also created a playroom for Julianna.

After they toured the home, Vivi paused beside the living room windows and looked out over the field and mountains. The setting sun glinted off the stream winding through the open field. Heath slid his arms around her waist from behind and rested his chin against her shoulder.

"So?"

"I love you," she said softly. She'd been about to say she loved the house, but it was Heath who made her love it.

She felt his lips curve against her neck. "Ditto," he

replied before he trailed kisses up her neck.

~The End~

Be sure to sign up for my newsletter! I promise - no spam! If you sign up, you'll get notices on new releases at discounted prices, information on upcoming books and great deals. Click here to sign up: http://jhcroix.com/page4/

Please enjoy the following excerpt from **A Catamount Christmas, Catamount Lion Shifters!**

Lion Lost & Found (Ghost Cat Shifters)

Chapter 1

Roxanne Morgan spun around and passed a sandwich over the counter, immediately turning to take the order of the next person in line.

"What'll it be?" she asked, her eyes quickly scanning the area beyond the counter. When there was no reply, she glanced up. Her heart stuttered and then lunged forward into a wild pounding.

"Hey Roxy," the man standing across the counter said.

Roxanne didn't find herself speechless very often, but at the moment, she couldn't seem to form a word. Max Stone stood in front of her—the one and only boy she'd ever loved and the boy who'd broken her heart when he left Catamount and left their love behind. Her eyes soaked him in—his mahogany brown hair, his amber eyes, and his lanky, muscled body. He wore a black down jacket, unzipped to reveal a charcoal gray shirt, and faded jeans. His eyes coasted over her. She felt bare and exposed and frantically tried to gather herself together inside.

Her cheeks felt hot, but she ignored it. She could do this. All she had to do was be polite. Her body was only reacting because she hadn't seen Max in so long. It was an echo of their past and nothing more. "Hey Max. Haven't seen you around in years," she finally replied, her words belying the turmoil she felt inside.

The truth was it had been precisely fifteen years since Max had been in Catamount. He had moved away with his mother after his father died in an accident at the mill in a nearby town. Roxanne and Max had started dating the year before, and she'd loved him in the way only youth allowed—head over heels infatuation mingled with a yearning to be together forever. The hopes of youth had kept her tendency toward cynicism at bay, and she'd flung herself into their relationship. On an afternoon when Max was supposed to come over, he'd called instead. In a conversation that lasted maybe five minutes, he told her that his father died, they were moving, and he broke up with her. She'd been too stunned to fully absorb what he said. A few days later when she managed to cobble together a coherent thought, she'd raced over to his house to try to say…something…and found the home he'd shared with his parents locked up. No one answered the door after she knocked for what felt like hours.

She'd swung between the emotional poles of grief, her own and for him about his father, and anger about the abrupt end of their relationship. She'd stuffed her grief away and done her damnedest to move on. The first few years after he left, she would occasionally wonder if she might hear from him, or if he would return to Catamount. She finally gave up hoping and wishing, but she never quite got over Max.

Now, he stood here before her. She twirled a pen

between her fingers and wondered what to do. A small part of her wanted to storm past him and not look back, just the way he'd left her all those years ago. She couldn't do that though because she owned Roxanne's Country Store. An arc of annoyance flashed through her. Max had shown up in the heart of her world.

"It's really good to see you, Roxy" Max said, cutting through her short walk down memory lane.

Max happened to be the only person who'd ever called her Roxy with any regularity. It chafed to hear him call her that now.

She willed herself to stay calm. Still struggling to form words sensibly, she nodded. She couldn't quite bring herself to say it was good to see him. A tornado of feelings swirled through her—confusion, hope, joy, anger, sadness and more. She was relieved when another customer stepped to the counter.

Hank Anderson, Catamount's police chief, leaned against the counter. "Hey Roxanne, can I get the usual today?"

Roxanne glanced to Hank. "Sure. Give me a sec." She forced a smile and turned away to pour a cup of coffee for Hank. At the moment, she would have given just about anything to have Becky here to help this morning. Becky would normally be here, but she'd called out sick with a nasty cold. Roxanne was reconsidering how relieved she'd been to not be exposed to whatever the hell Becky had. She'd sounded like she was on the verge of death when she called, so Roxanne had happily supported her staying home until she was better. But now, with Max here, Roxanne didn't have any back up, so she couldn't busy herself in the back. She had no choice but to stay here and somehow fumble through the next few minutes. She prayed Max wouldn't stay long. As she fitted the lid over Hank's coffee, she heard him start talking to Max and anxiety tightened in her chest.

"Max Stone? Damn, haven't seen you around in years! How are ya?" Hank asked.

Roxanne turned back to face them, gripping Hank's coffee tightly in her hand. Max grinned over at Hank. "Hey Hank, it's good to see you. It might have been a long time, but I'm back to stay."

A tremor ran through her, and her stomach felt hollow. Max was back to stay? So many questions tumbled through her mind, she couldn't think clearly. She mentally shook herself. It had been fifteen years. She was long past her youthful love for him, and he'd clearly never felt the same way. If he had, she didn't see how he could have left things between them the way he did.

Max and Hank were still talking when she looked back over and took the few steps to the counter. She set Hank's coffee down and slid it over. "Here you go"

Hank snagged it and took a gulp. "Ahh. Perfect." He pulled his wallet out, glancing between Roxanne and Max as he did. "Did you two stay in touch all these years?" Hank asked.

His question was innocent enough, but it sent a flash of anger through Roxanne. She wasn't up for nosy questions. She busied herself taking the ten-dollar bill Hank handed over and getting him change from the register, her ears perked to see how Max responded to Hank's question.

"Unfortunately not," Max replied. "Things were a little hectic that first year after my dad died, and I wasn't thinking too clearly."

Roxanne couldn't stop herself from looking over to Max. His amber eyes caught hers. "Roxanne was the first person I looked for when I got here, so I'm hoping we'll have time to catch up."

Hank chuckled. "Roxanne's Country Store here is still the heart and soul of Catamount. She's done her family proud running it the way she does." Hank took another swallow of coffee. "Anyway, good to see you, Max. If you need anything, just stop by. Where you staying?"

"My mom never sold our old house, so I'm planning to renovate it."

Hank pushed away from the counter. "Well, you've got your work cut out for you. Don't think anybody's been there since you all left."

Something flashed in Max's eyes. Once upon a time, Roxanne might have thought it was pain, but she wouldn't know right now. Though her body was spinning with heat and the familiarity of Max's presence, her mind was bolting doors around her heart and insisting she not go thinking she knew him the way she once did.

"I'm sure I do. I plan to head up there in a little bit to take a look. Good to see you, Hank."

"If you need any help, let me know and I'm sure I can round up a few kids from the high school to help out with the land clearing. They're young and too strong to worry about their backs yet," Hank said as he lifted his coffee cup in a farewell and turned away.

Max turned back to the counter. For a long moment, he didn't say anything. He simply looked at her, his eyes coasting over her face and dipping down before returning. Her cheeks heated when his gaze met hers again. "I'm guessing this feels kind of out of the blue for you, huh?"

Her heart in her throat, Roxanne nodded.

Max curled his hands on the edge of the counter. "I have enough sense to know now probably isn't a great time to talk, but I just need you to know I'm sorry. I couldn't have stopped my mom from up and leaving Catamount the way we did right after my dad died, but I shouldn't have broken things off with you the way I did."

Another customer approached the counter. Gail
Anderson, Hank's wife, stepped to Max's side. "I just saw
Hank on his way out," Gail said, not bothering with a
perfunctory greeting.

With her mind spinning over what Max had just
said, Roxanne turned to Gail, barely able to think. She must
have managed to nod because Gail huffed. "I told him I
was only running a few minutes behind!" Gail's blue eyes
snapped. Gail and Hank were long-time Catamount
residents, both born and raised here, and married straight
out of high school. Hank was the police chief and Gail was
a retired schoolteacher. Gail glanced to her side, her eyes
widening. "Max Stone?"

*Oh. My. God. Just how many of these moments am I
going to have to survive? Well, Max's family was here for a
long time before they left. Anyone that knew him is going to
be startled to see him. You'd better get used to this.*
Roxanne mentally sighed as she tried to marshal her
thoughts. *It might mean nothing that Max said he shouldn't
have broken things off the way he did. He might not have
felt the way you did anyway, he just feels bad about how he
handled it. Don't go thinking it's anything other than that.
Just act normal and get through this.*

Roxanne cued in to the conversation between Max
and Gail. "I decided to move back last summer after my
mom died. Her sister was the reason we moved to Virginia
and she died the year before, so there was nothing left
holding me there. I missed Catamount the entire time we
were gone, so I decided it was time to come home."

Gail looked between Max and Roxanne, her eyes
considering. She appeared about to say something, but she
stayed quiet for several beats. "Well, it's nice to have you
back. I missed your mother. I'm sorry to hear she passed

away."

Max nodded solemnly. "I wish she'd had a chance to get back here before she died."

Gail nodded firmly. "It is what it is. Everyone will be glad to know you're here." She turned to Roxanne. "I was supposed to meet Hank for coffee, but since he couldn't be bothered wait, I'll get some to go."

Roxanne felt like she was in a surreal dream. On autopilot, she swung around and poured a cup of coffee for Gail. Moments later, Gail was walking through the deli and down the aisle to the front door.

When Roxanne turned back to Max, she forced herself to keep it light because she couldn't deal with anything else right now. "What can I get for you?" she asked, her words coming out smoothly only because she'd said them thousands of times.

***

Max looked over at Roxanne and tamped down the urge to leap over the counter and pull her into his arms. She stood there before him, her blonde hair pulled back in a haphazard ponytail, loose curls escaping and framing her heart-shaped face. Her blue eyes were as gorgeous as he remembered—wide eyes that tipped up at the corners, the blue so rich, he could lose himself in it. Not a day had passed since he left when he didn't think about her, and here she stood before him—taking his breath away. Fifteen years later, she'd filled out and her figure was all curves—generous breasts, an hourglass dip at her waist, and lush hips. She emanated a strength and power she hadn't had back when they were young.

Max had so much to say, yet now clearly was not the time or place. Roxanne's Country Store was bustling. The deli area had customers seated at tables scattered

169

throughout the small area. The rest of the store, a mix of groceries, hardware and just about everything, had customers meandering through the aisles as they filled shopping baskets. This place held so many memories for him, it was almost overwhelming.

Fifteen years ago, he came home from school to find his mother had already packed up everything in his bedroom and announced they were moving to Virginia. That morning, his father had died in an accident at the paper mill in a neighboring town. Max was emotionally reeling and didn't know what to think about anything. He still didn't know why he'd broken up with Roxanne when he called her to tell her what happened. He'd replayed that conversation in his mind over and over again. The only conclusion he could come to was he'd been in such shock, he thought everything was ending at once.

He'd stumbled through the next few weeks, twisted and turned in the emotional turmoil of his father's death, his mother's grief and trying to adjust to living somewhere new. He'd been born and raised in Catamount, Maine—a shifter stronghold and the founding community of all shifters. Being born into a family of shifters, when they moved to Virginia, he'd been forced to adjust to a life of secrecy. Until the year before his mother died, he'd never quite understood why they left Catamount. The years passed and he never forgot Roxanne. Every so often, he'd thought about calling her. Once, he actually did. Her mother had answered and told him in no uncertain terms that he'd broken Roxanne's heart. Whether or not she told Roxanne he called, he didn't know. He'd never gathered the nerve to call Roxanne again.

He looked over at Roxanne. A sharp pain slashed through him to see the guarded expression in her eyes. He wanted to make things right with her. Now. He started to say something when yet another customer approached the counter. Blessedly, whoever this was didn't seem to know him. They ordered a sandwich and went to sit at one of the small round tables. Roxanne caught his eyes. "If you'd like to order, now would be the time."

There was a sharp edge to her voice. Max fought back the urge to ask her if they could talk now. "Right. I can see you're busy. I'll take a coffee."

She spun away and stepped behind another counter to make the requested sandwich. She called out when it was ready, handing it over to the customer, before she got his coffee ready. When she slid the bright blue paper coffee cup across the counter, his heart gave a hard kick. He remembered spending many afternoons here with her. She was still using the same cups her parents used when they ran the store. She was busy doing something at the register. He waited, hoping she would pause. When she didn't, he moved to stand in front of the register.

"Roxy?"

Her eyes whipped up. For a flash, he saw pain and something else there, but she quickly shuttered it. He forged ahead. "Look, I'm hoping we can talk. Soon. I missed you. More than I can even say. I'll go now because I know you're working, but maybe I could take you out for dinner or something?"

Roxanne stared at him for so long, uncertainty began to slide through him. He heard her take a deep breath and close her eyes. When she opened them, she looked right at him. "Okay. Fine. We might as well get this over with. Tonight's no good because Becky's out sick, so I'll be here until closing. How about tomorrow?"

He couldn't keep from smiling. "Tomorrow's perfect. Six o'clock work?"

She nodded slowly. He reached over and grabbed a

small pad of paper and a pen sitting by the register. He quickly jotted down his cell number. "Just so you have it."

***

Roxanne watched Max leave. He wove through the tables and headed down the center aisle, his lean body ambling, yet giving off a sense of leashed power. His dark hair glinted in the sun cast through the front windows. He looked back when he reached the door, and she felt as if there was an invisible current between them. Even from across the room, she felt that shimmering connection. She forced her eyes away and looked up at the next customer, wondering if she'd gone and lost her mind by so quickly agreeing to have dinner with him.

Coming soon!
A Catamount Christmas

Go here to sign up for information on new releases: http://jhcroix.com/page4/

Thank you for reading Lion Lost & Found (Ghost Cat Shifters)! I hope you enjoyed the story. If so, you can help other readers find my books in a variety of ways.

1) Write a review!

2) Sign up for my newsletter, so you can receive information about upcoming new releases at http://jhcroix.com/page4/

3) Follow me on Twitter at https://twitter.com/JHCroix

4) Like my Facebook page at https://www.facebook.com/jhcroix

5) Like and follow my Amazon Author page at https://amazon.com/author/jhcroix

J.H. Croix

Catamount Lion Shifters

Protected Mate

Chosen Mate

Fated Mate

Destined Mate

Ghost Cat Shifters

The Lion Within

Lion Lost & Found

Diamond Creek Alaska Novels

When Love Comes

Follow Love

Love Unbroken

Love Untamed

Tumble Into Love

Last Frontier Lodge Novels

Christmas on the Last Frontier

Love at Last

Just This Once

Falling Fast

174

Acknowledgments

No book would be complete without my personal hero cheering me on and sharing every success. Laura Kingsley continues to edit like a champ and insists I jump a little higher each time. Once again, Claire Tan at CT Cover Creations created a stunning cover. Gracious thanks and hugs to my readers for your enthusiastic support!

J.H. Croix

Author Biography

Bestselling author J. H. Croix lives in a small town in the
historical farmlands of Maine with her husband and two
spoiled dogs. Croix writes sexy contemporary romance and
steamy paranormal romance with strong independent
women and rugged alpha men who aren't afraid to show
some emotion. Her love for quirky small-towns and the
characters that inhabit them shines through in her writing.
Take a walk on the wild side of romance with her
bestselling novels!

CPSIA information can be obtained
at www.ICGtesting.com
Printed in the USA
FSOW01n2027050617
35057FS